A DANGEROUS
PLACE TO LOVE

M'landan leaned back, his eyes on her face. The room was hot with their vibrations.

Oddly, it was the coolness of his skin that Darenga noticed, the coolness of his skin, and the light fragile structure of his body, like some fantastic bird that stood with folded wings as she caressed it. She pressed against him.

"Let me do this for you . . . and for me," M'landan whispered.

His fingers came swiftly down around her wrists, locking her palms against his. The laanva poured into her hands and raced burning up her arms exploding against her heart . . .

Suddenly the screens were flung aside and the deep tone M'landan had begun died in his throat. The room exploded with Laatam's scream of outrage and Trolon's manic cry, "EVERYTHING IS DEFILED!"

Other Avon books by
Francine Mezo

THE FALL OF WORLDS

Coming Soon

NO EARTHLY SHORE

UNLESS SHE BURN

FRANCINE MEZO

▲ AVON
PUBLISHERS OF BARD, CAMELOT AND DISCUS BOOKS

Unless she burn.

UNLESS SHE BURN is an original publication of Avon Books.
This work has never before appeared in book form.

AVON BOOKS
A division of
The Hearst Corporation
959 Eighth Avenue
New York, New York 10019

Copyright © 1981 by Francine Mezo
Published by arrangement with the author
Library of Congress Catalog Card Number: 80-68412
ISBN: 0-380-76968-9

First Avon Printing, January, 1981

AVON TRADEMARK REG. U.S. PAT. OFF. AND IN
OTHER COUNTRIES, MARCA REGISTRADA, HECHO EN U.S.A.

Printed in the U.S.A.

It is with fire that blacksmiths iron subdue
Unto fair form, the image of their thought:
Nor without the fire hath any artist wrought
Gold to its utmost purity of hue.
Nay, nor the unmatched phoenix lives anew,
Unless she burn.

MICHELANGELO; *Sonnet 59*

Chapter 1

At first the creaking of cart wheels, then the solemn procession winding down through the narrow streets past the golden domes and fragile silver edifices of the city, toward the plain beyond, only the sound of cart wheels and the slow shuffling of the thousand marchers. At the head of the procession went two tall figures dressed, as the whole company was dressed, in hooded robes tinted gold by the rusty sky. Behind the figures walked a solitary priest in the same measured pace, and after him the people. The priest was slightly taller than the others, well over seven feet, and slender. His hood was banded in dark purple. He walked with his arms folded, the hands hidden in the long sleeves of his robe, his head bent forward so the edges of the hood concealed his face.

The two leaders and the priest reached the level ground and stood waiting quietly for the rest of the city's inhabitants to make the descent. Beyond the juncture of slope and tableland where they waited the plain stretched to the horizon in a broad band of islands, floating away on the emerald sand that glittered under the planet's two suns. On the purple-tufted island grew L'M'dia—life and eventual death for the M'dian people who gathered now for *tlee haaranu*, the little harvest.

The plant was nearly four meters high but had a look of slender fragility like the people who tended and depended on it. Each pale stock, with its dark, lethal ring at the base, supported a golden sphere some sixty centimeters in diameter. A delicate web of black veins laced each globe. Midway on the stock were four fanning black branches, finely structured, with small oval buds in tiny cups at the tip of each twig, the buds being the focus of *tlee haaranu*, a cyclic activity in the religious life of the people of Ilanu.

The priest, perceiving all the people arrived and waiting,

raised his head, his face becoming visible in the shadow of his hood, the eyes first, great bowls holding the black ocular fluid and dimmed by a thin nictitating membrane which closed down immediately to protect the delicate substance from the suns' radiation. His nose was broad, rounding over into an upper lip and producing, in the expression of his mouth, a long and faintly quizzical line. The great liquid eyes and the odd curve of his mouth marked his features with gentleness and patience, qualities reflected in the faces around him.

The small white sun stood just above the far horizon where the Yarbeen, the narrow axial shadow cast by the planet's ring, lay eternally on the planet. The priest lifted his head toward the sun.

"*Sai Baandla!*" His voice rang out in the singing language of the M'dians as he invoked the name of the white dwarf. "I ask thy blessing on *tlee haaranu.*"

His voice was baritone, with a clear and haunting tonality resonant with emotion. Now he raised his hands, slender hands with three long nailless fingers and opposing thumbs, holding the palms up so the concentric rings of small skin perforations were toward the sun.

"I ask thee to draw out the sacred laanva that I may know thy blessing is on this harvest."

He tilted back his head, and the light fell on his face, on skin faintly iridescent, like the petal of a flower viewed in a jeweler's glass. The protective scrim now drew back from his eyes as he stared directly into the sun's rays. "I ask thy blessing," he sang.

"We ask it, *Sai Baandla,*" the people responded in a low, sweet chant.

"I ask thy blessing."

"We ask it, *Sai Baandla.*"

"I ask thy blessing."

The alternate chant between priest and people intensified, became deeper.

"*We ask it*, Sai Baandla."

"*I ask thy blessing.*"

The small perforations in the palms of the priest began to glisten. He twisted his hands in a smooth, ritualistic motion, cupping them down in front of him. The song of the crowd abruptly became a low vibrating tone. In the air was the faint odor of honey.

8

The two figures who had led the procession swung a long purple cloth under the hands of the priest. Now he closed the inner lid of his eyes, shutting out the dangerous rays of the two suns. His cupped hands were filling with a thin liquid, and he balanced them carefully as he moved forward to one of the islands, which had been encircled by a group of the people. His assistants moved with him, holding the cloth beneath his hands as he stepped up into the thick purple grass. He approached one of the plants, held out his hands.

"L'M'dia, we are blessed," he sang.

"We are blessed," echoed the people of the city in the same low tone.

"L'M'dia, *tlee haaranu* is blessed."

The crowd: "*Sai Baandla* has blessed our harvest."

"This is the fluid of our bodies. We pass it to thee as we will in the final days of *Maleelonos*." The priest slowly poured the liquid from his hands over the buds of each branch of the stalk. The purple cloth moved below his hands, absorbing any liquid that fell.

"We are blessed," he sang out in a swiftly rising melodic line that was pursued by the voices around him. "All our generations are blessed!" It ended in a sharp unsatisfied phrase that hovered on the air in the soft insistent tone of the chorus.

The priest began to pluck the buds, dropping them one by one into the cloth as the unresolved tone grew louder. The buds fell against the material, jostling to a center dark with spilled liquid. The assistant at his left moved the cloth slightly, and he glanced into her eyes, saw the expression there and knew she was being stirred by the sweet odor from his hands. He looked away, plucked the last of the buds, let them fall, pressed his hands against the cloth. Then he turned, raised his arms, and sang, "We are blessed," twice, in his ringing baritone, and the chorus answered, the second line ending in a joyful crescendo as the people moved forward into the fields in a swift change of mood from reverence to excitement. The carts were wheeled ahead between the islands, the woven bins rocking gently against the sides. The M'dians spread out in groups and in pairs, picking the buds into the aprons they had made of the fronts of their robes.

"Shall I bring you the cloth, M'landan?" the priest's

assistant asked in the sweet-sad lilt that characterized her song. Her eyes still held the expression he had seen a few moments before.

"Thank you, no, Tlaima," he answered gently. "I'm going back to the haruund now. I'll take it with me."

She gave up the cloth to him with its sacred buds folded inside, the cloth that would lie beneath his head at *Maleelonos*, at his death, at all their deaths when their bodies would be placed in caskets of oil by children not yet born.

He turned away, knowing she would soon be in the islands gathering this first pleasant harvest, that she would, in the following hours, be joining in communion with one of the males of the city, sharing the experience he was forbidden because his body was the reservoir of his people's generations, and the fluid was measured and finite.

He stepped down from the island onto the green sand and, with the cloth in his hands, started up the slope to the deserted city. After mounting a little way he stopped and, for a long moment, looked back over the plain where his people moved among the plants, and he could hear little scraps of song as they called to one another; he looked out across the islands of L'M'dia to the dark maroon shadow of the Yarbeen before he turned and continued up a narrow street of the city which led to the haruund, the community complex. Then, once more, he glanced back. Now climbing the hill behind him were four figures, the Greynin: the Group of Conscience. He gazed at them thoughtfully, then went on into the main building of the complex.

The sloping corridors of the haruund were narrow; if he had extended either of his arms halfway he could have touched the wall. All passages in their buildings, and all the streets, were narrow, close, safe. A habit of construction from dark eons past.

He went past doorways hung with staggered fiber screens woven in patterns that were variations on L'M'dia, finally turning in at one removed from the others. The room was a translucent and glowing oval. He crossed the thick fiber flooring to a large round jar and knelt down to open it. Through a window opening the white sun shone in, and he briefly held his arms so the light lay across the cloth. Then he laid it inside the jar, made a sweeping circular movement over it with his hands, and then replaced the lid.

He rose, made his way out through the whispering screens.

They were standing quietly in the gathering room when he entered.

"We would speak with you, M'landan."

M'landan pushed back his hood as the others had, and slipped his hands into his sleeves. "As you wish, Trolon," he answered in the same formal melody the other male had used. "But why has the Greynin formed to speak with me?"

"We have two matters to bring to you, if you will permit," Trolon responded.

"Say, Trolon."

"We're concerned that you haven't chosen the Chaeya."

"Have you chosen a mate?" M'landan countered softly.

"I don't carry the seed of our generations," Trolon answered.

"Your choice should be first, M'landan," sang one of the females in a vibrant contralto.

"You all will bear my children, Laatam."

"Yes," the other female reminded him quickly, "but the Chaeya bears the priest for the next generation."

"Quanti is right," sang the fourth member, Samar. "The selection is important; it must be the most compatible mating for you. And we can't make our choices until you do."

Trolon raised his hand and drew the finger of his other hand around the circle of perforations on his palm—a gesture of emphasis. "We request that you make your selection," he said.

"Have you set a time on me?" M'landan asked with a slight harshness.

"We don't wish to sound impatient, M'landan," Laatam said in a slow soothing tone, "but you seem to delay."

M'landan looked at her, assessing the harmonics in her phrase. Finally, he answered, "I will make a choice, and it will be soon." The truth rang in his voice, and the four made a slight circular movement with their right hands, indicating that they accepted his answer.

"And now the other matter . . . ?"

"We would speak about the One-Who-Far-Journeys, my priest." Again, formality.

The priest made a motion with his hand, signalling Trolon to continue.

"Her mind is clouded. She has been teaching, in this room, certain things—"

"I interrupt," M'landan said politely. "She does not teach. She speaks of things she knows about the heavens, and only when she is asked."

Trolon's eyes were unreflective for an instant. "My priest," he went on, "she speaks of Great Yamth and Shining Baandla as globes of fire. She has said that Yamth is dying, that our jewel Baandla will go dark. She makes these blasphemies and—with respect I must point out— you say nothing."

Laatam said, "I've witnessed your silence myself, my priest."

"What would you want me to say, Laatam? She has beliefs, as we do. Shall we demand her silence in our fear that our gods are not real?"

The group reacted with a ripple of discordancy.

"We didn't say that, M'landan," Trolon replied. "Our faith is strong. But if she does not recognize our gods, she must be sent away. That is our law."

"Are you telling me what our laws are?"

"We consider why you do not try to show her the true way," Trolon replied.

"She knows what our beliefs are, Trolon. I don't look for converts. My role is priest to my people, father of the next generation. I'll not silence her when she answers questions asked by our people."

"But, my priest," sang Quanti, "the things she tells create confusion in the minds of some. They know she came through the heavens. They saw her great ship hanging like a daystar in our skies while she and her people walked among us and spoke to us in our language. They saw them riding the air on machines. And they listen to her now because these things were wonderful and they begin to doubt what they should not."

"Tell me their names, Quanti, and I'll speak to them and judge the depth of their uncertainty."

"I . . . don't know their names, M'landan."

"It is a general murmur we hear," Laatam said. "We hesitate to name one rather than another when both may have listened and expressed doubt, yet one may have ultimately kept to the truth while the other did not. We would ask that you prevent this doubt, my priest. Can she not be

12

asked to refrain from these long responses? Surely she would grant us that courtesy. We have asked nothing else of her."

There had been a tense thinness to her voice that vibrated unpleasantly, and M'landan had turned his head slightly so the effect on his ear membrane was lessened. "You do keep in your memory," he responded, "that it was her people who brought a cure that saved this generation from the death and deformity all our past generations had suffered?"

"I do not forget, M'landan. But may I say respectfully that we have welcomed her here when her own kind would not—"

"I interrupt," said the priest. "Her people, those under her command and guidance, did not wish for her to leave. She left them because she didn't have long to live, and because there had been too many battles and too much destruction. She wanted no more of it. She couldn't return to her world. She wanted only to die in peace." He stopped. His own voice was becoming tense, the notes discordant.

"We would wonder what agency has prolonged her life," Trolon asked in the uncomfortable silence. "It is four years past the time she was to die." This long run of notes was carefully controlled, and yet there was an unpleasant strain on the melody.

"You said if she didn't receive the treatments that kept her ageless, she would die quickly." This was Laatam.

"And she continues to live," said Quanti.

"To mock our religion!" Samar cried.

"Would you have her die to satisfy your complaints?" M'landan asked in an ugly coda to the strident counterpoint directed at him.

The four stared at him rigidly, their eyes dull and frozen.

He silently rebuked himself. Then to each one he said, "*Mlo saindla,*" *forgive me,* and lay his hand on the side of each of their heads in turn, covering the ear membrane. The effect was immediate and calming. The four leaders replaced their hands into their sleeves and stood waiting for him to speak.

"I'll discuss this with her," he said.

"She isn't in the city."

"I know, Trolon. She's in the Yarbeen."

"Eating flesh," said Quanti. The sound was thick with

revulsion, but tagged with a quick apologetic note at the end; she had not meant to say it that way.

M'landan answered kindly, "L'M'dia is poison to her. She must eat what foods she can find that her body will tolerate." He looked at them. "Is there any other matter you would like to speak with me about?"

"You have answered us, M'landan. We are satisfied."

The priest brought his hands up, drew a slow circle above them.

"All is within," they responded, and walked slowly away through the screens.

The priest raised his hood, pulled the banded edge around his face, and turned to stare out the wall opening toward the dark shadow line beyond the plain.

Chapter 2

The woman squatted before a fire in the deep maroon shadow of the Yarbeen, gazing vacantly at the flames as she ate with slow methodical bites from the long stickful of meat she held in her hand. Her long copper-colored hair was tied back, but wisps of it moved against her face with the soft honey-scented breeze that blew in through the islands. Every so often she would brush the hair away with the back of her hand. Even that gesture emphasized the concentration that marked her pose.

She wore a M'dian robe, but on a large rock nearby lay a bronze-colored cloak—the only vestment that would have identified her as having been a fleet captain, the commander of a galactic ship that had led a battle, had won a war, and then been trapped on the far side of a collapsing fold of time and space. She used the cloak as blanket and coat, as ground cover and awning, whatever the need of the moment required it to be. She had no sentimental attachment to it; it was merely useful.

She continued to eat at the tiny rodent-like animals which had taken her so long to catch, devouring each carcass on the skewer; bones, entrails—all of it was nourishment and the only source of calcium available to her on the planet.

There was still half a skewer left when she heard a sound and looked up in the act of chewing, looked toward the islands, like an animal interrupted by birds or smaller animals that occasioned no fear. She saw the familiar figure and slowly lowered the skewer away from her mouth.

"Areia," M'landan said, "may I speak with you?" The revulsion was there in his voice as he saw what she held in her hand, saw the oily sheen around her mouth as she had lifted her head toward him, smelled with his sensitive nostrils the odor of roasted flesh.

She heard this in his voice and saw him swallow quickly several times before he turned his head away. She glanced down at the skewer, then made a swift trench in the sand with her fist and dropped it in, covering it over. From a fold in her robe she drew a cloth, wiped her hands and face, buried the cloth as she had the meat. A water container and a pack lay close at hand, and she took them up as she came to her feet, and with another look at the priest who stood with his face averted, unable to speak, she retreated behind a large boulder.

It was several minutes before she reappeared, but by then the odor had dissipated and he had regained his composure.

"I try to keep away from everyone when I'm eating meat," she said in M'dian; a neutral song. She dropped the pack and the water container back on the ground.

"You show us every consideration. I intruded."

There was no trace about her of meat; no odor, however faint, drifted to his nostrils now. He watched as she dug at the coals of the fire.

"I will have something vegetable, though, if you don't mind." She plucked out a long tuber and opened it on a rock. The steam curled up, and he caught a bright tangy odor.

"Yes, please. Go ahead and eat."

"Is this smell offensive to you, M'landan?" she asked, looking over at him with her clear eyes that were the color of the M'dian soil.

"No, not at all. I like it."

"On my homeworld this aroma comes from a fruit we call raspberry, although the fruit looks nothing like this." She would have added that it tasted like a mollusk called abalone, but didn't want to upset him any more than he already was. "What did you want to talk to me about?"

"Not now. Please finish your meal."

"Would you like some water?"

"Yes, I would appreciate that."

"I'd think so; that's a long dry walk."

He leaned forward, holding his hand out so she could place the small bowl in his palm.

For an instant the bowl wavered as she looked down at the circle of perforations. Then her eyes lifted to his, the bowl was in his palm, and he was drawing it back to his mouth with an unsteady hand. He lowered his long tubular tongue delicately into the water and drank. Darenga looked away, tossed the piece of tuber she had been about to eat into the fire and poured water for herself instead, and sat sipping at it. There was a long silence. With a small vagrant twist of the breeze came the far-off lilt of a joyful voice.

"You began some sort of harvest today," she said.

"*Tlee haaranu,*" he answered. "The buds are being gathered."

"The M'dians gone a-Maying."

He tilted his head politely.

"An ancient orgy," she said, dismissing the subject. "Did you officiate?"

"Yes. Baandla's blessing is required for the harvest."

"I'm sorry I missed it. You're very impressive at that sort of thing."

He didn't answer because he had caught the slight hint of mockery in her voice.

She thought, *I'm getting too cynical; he doesn't deserve that.* She told him, "*Mlo saindla.* But you are impressive, you know," and this time the note was genuine.

Still, he didn't respond, and thinking there might be a lingering odor in the air that was contributing to his silence she said, "Let's go where it's a little more comfortable."

She picked up the water container and her cloak. "Bring the bowls, will you?" He obediently scooped them up and followed her through the rocks and into a small depressed area formed by a rough circle of upright boulders. There was only one opening, and the ground sloped away from it into the flattened drift of green sand that formed the floor.

"My parlor," she said, and snapped her cloak briskly, then let it sail to the ground. She set the water container on the edge of the bronze cloak, then sank down beside it. "Sit down, M'landan."

She watched him settle himself lightly, like a balloon coming to earth, his robe spreading about him. He pushed his hood back—relaxed, finally—and looked up toward the entranceway. It opened like a keyhole on the dark air. There, through the twilight of the Yarbeen, the stars shone faintly, and all above the wall of rock was the same dim roof of stars widening into space; a natural planetarium. He turned his head to her, and her eyes slid away from his glance.

He began a low melody, a murmur of understanding, but she said, "Don't!" quick and sharp in her own language, and he was silent.

In the pause that followed she took the bowls from where he had laid them and slowly filled them, placed one in front of each of them, straightened, looked at him again. "Well, tell me now why you hiked twenty kilometers across the sand on a holiday just to see me."

He was a moment drawing his thoughts together, but finally answered, "I had a conversation with the Greynin this sunfall."

"Mmm," she asknowledged with a nod. "And what did they say to you?"

She listened thoughtfully as he told her their concern about her remarks in the gathering room, and he was too honest to leave out the strident exchange over her prolonged life. She sat running her fingertips around the edge of her bowl.

"I don't know why I haven't started into Life'send, but you might tell them there are times I would like to get it over with myself. Not knowing is . . . tedious for me as well." Her head came up. "As for the other thing—I hadn't realized my conversations in the gathering room were creating a problem in faith. I think it might be better if I stay out here—away from the city—"

"No!" he said. And then, less harshly, "No. I gave my permission for you to stay in the haruund, and no one will reverse that. Your home is there now."

She laughed softly. "My home is where my cloak is, M'landan. But I'll stay there if you want me to; if you don't think they'll be antagonized by me. There is a certain justification in their complaints, though; I have been a little free with my . . . opinions."

She had wavered between "beliefs," which would have patronized him, and "knowledge," which would have seemed arrogant, if truthful, and had settled somewhere between.

He understood the compromise. "I do not wish your silence. Their fears are not my own."

"I know you're putting no strictures on me. Just say

you've presented me with the facts and, after weighing them, I've decided on prudence in all matters that touch on religion." Her crooked, wistful smile faded almost before it materialized, and she looked down at her bowl, ran her thumb around the top.

"The Greynin discussed another matter with me," he said quietly, and she glanced up at the curious note she heard in his voice.

"Oh?"

"I will be selecting the Chaeya soón."

"Chaeya—that's the Loved One, isn't it? the mother of the next generation's priest?"

"Yes."

She nodded. "I don't know very much about your mating customs; your elders didn't have much to say to the research teams on that subject—"

"It is a very private matter."

"Of course. And I'm not questioning you about it now. I meant to say that even though I don't understand the process, I do wish you well in the choosing. Have you selected someone yet, or is that a question out of proper form?"

"Necessity makes the choice." The odd note again that the Implanted Translation Unit in her brain faltered over. "It will be either Tlaima—"

"Well, that would keep the business in the family."

"—or Laatam."

"Mmmhmm. One for her gentleness, the other for her strength. Not an easy choice, M'landan. How will necessity make it? Or do I detect an equivocation on the word *choice*?"

"I will make the choice because it has become necessary for me to do so."

"Ah." Her thumb went around the rim of the bowl again. "Will there be a ceremony—? Of course there will be—what kind?"

"Long."

She laughed. "How does a priest get married when he's the only priest?"

"We call it *shoma*, the joining, and the priest of Klada will come—"

"—and you'll go to Klada when *he* goes through shoma. I see. Very communal. Well, I will want to see you joined in this long ceremony, M'landan, to see how you take to being on the other side of a prayer." She raised her bowl to him. "To the prospective groom," she said, "and to the bride, whichever one she turns out to be."

He watched silently as she took a drink, her eyes glittering at him. Then he reached over and lay his hand on the bowl, pressing it gently toward her lap. "You have been in pain again," he said quietly.

Her eyes lost their glitter, and she looked down. "I've had some pain lately, yes," she finally replied.

"And the hallucinations . . . ?"

"I haven't come to you, M'landan—"

"No. I have come to you. Please answer me. Are you still able to hallucinate?"

"No."

They were both silent across the brief distance that separated them.

"M'landan, you ask me these things, and your language prevents me from lying to you." She hesitated, gave him a long, searching look. "You must know I'm ashamed of the demands I made on you. The contact we had still disturbs you, and I . . . don't want to cause you this kind of difficulty. Besides," she told him, "I've had a lifetime of training in metabolism control. I've gotten a little rusty in pain suppression, but I can handle it again. It just takes practice. And concentration. And discipline. . . ." Her voice faded. She took a breath. "It's a question of discipline—" She stopped, hearing the false tones and disharmony in the song she was attempting.

M'landan moved slightly. In her effort to convince him she had laid her hand on his arm, and in concentrating on weaving the proper melody she had been steadily increasing her grip until now it threatened the hollow bone in his arm. He lifted his other hand and laid it against her ear. "I understand," he sang softly. "Be comforted."

Her eyes dilated suddenly, and she released the pressure on his arm. "*Mlo saindla*," she said.

He drew back his hand and rested it in his lap. "What should I forgive?"

She shook her head. "I don't know," she replied. "There's so much. . . ." She reached forward and lay her hands along his throat. "Too much, perhaps."

The warmth of her hands, the pressure of her fingertips against his skin, was soothing now, and gentle, and he

20

found her closeness relaxing. But now she sank back, changed her position so she was half reclining, her torso braced against her arm. She looked away from him.

"That was enjoyable," he said, in case she might have thought him offended, for even now she was not fully aware of the intricacies of his religion and the customs of his people.

She turned her head back then and gazed at him from the depths of some unmeasurable need that he could only half understand. He moved forward, drawn as much by the pressure of her touch that still lingered on his throat as by what he perceived in her eyes.

"Will this violate your laws?" she asked, lying back against the cloak, her hands closing around his face as he came down beside her.

He understood. Now, as she spoke, the soft harmonics, the undertones of insistence, the tension of communion was in her voice. A sudden fire erupted in his arms. From deep inside him, the word came, involuntarily and barely audible: *Chaeya*. But she felt the sad, anguished melody breathe against her hair, and her hands fell instantly away from him. When he lifted his head to question this motion, he saw her hands where they lay exposed on the bronze cloth, the fingers half curved above the glistening palms, and he moved forward.

She felt him reaching for her hands, the movement registering slowly on the network of her own sudden needs, and before she could whisper "Don't!" his palms had already slid against hers, the three long fingers curling like tendrils around her own, straightening them, arching the palms tightly against the perforations in his skin.

"*Mlo saindla*, my gods," he said in a low voice, "I do this in secrecy and darkness."

And she went rigid as the hot liquid gushed into her hands, and with it the pain streaming up through her arms and bursting into her chest. She lay smothering in the heavy odor of honey, drowning in it as she tried to catch her breath. His voice murmured down in waves of fragrance. Then it was over. The pain was gone, her lungs expanded, and she sat up, giddy. He had come to his feet and was standing above her, pulling the hood up around his face.

"M'landan—"

"I must go." He turned, started up the slope to the entrance.

"M'landan, please!"

He hesitated, but went on quickly through the entrance.

She moved as fast as she could through the stones and out in the direction he had taken.

"M'landan!"

He was already some thirty meters away, but he stopped, came around in a whirl of robes. "Stay!" he called. "Please do not follow me!"

But she did, and he turned and began running, skimming the ground as lightly as if he would suddenly fly into the air.

"Goddamn you!" she cried out, knowing she couldn't catch him. "Why are you doing this!" She stopped.

There was no answer in the breeze that blew in from the islands. She stood listening, trying to bind up the anger and frustration with the tatters of neglected discipline, acutely aware that she should return to the safety of her camp before the hallucinations began. But instead she moved slowly into the fields, and out of the shadow of the Yarbeen where the islands lay quiet in the reddish light with only a sigh now and then as the breeze ruffled the long purple grass.

After some moments of aimless searching she started back, and then, hearing a low moan, traced it to where M'landan lay doubled up on the sand. She dropped down beside him just as a spasm went through his body. His head jerked back, opening his face to the light. He was not aware of her. His eyes were dull, then suddenly brilliant, glinting in the white sunlight. The membrane slid down, trembled, drew partly up. Abruptly he rolled over and would have thrust his face and half-opened eyes into the sand if she hadn't grabbed his hood and held up his head. She sat with her arms around him so that, in his thrashing, he wouldn't injure himself. It wasn't difficult: For all his tremendous size, he might have weighed 150 pounds. And as she held him he alternately sang and called painfully in short bursts of melody across a scale she had hardly imagined possible.

She stayed by him, restraining the erratic movements that might break the fragile bones or clog his lungs with sand or destroy the delicate jelly of his eyes. And all the while the strange wild notes beat at her eardrums, striking chords of unrelated response in her, as if some mad surgeon probed at the centers of her brain.

Finally he grew quiet and lay silently on his back, his arms folded. She pulled the hood around his face so the still half-opened eyes would be shaded, and then sat back, her hands resting on her knees.

From somewhere to her left there was a sudden faintly heard but brilliant chime of metal. And simultaneously the delicate agony that overlay all her waking moments and hung a dark vibration in her sleep was gone. She looked toward the direction the familiar sound had come from.

A man approached through the islands, a dark form in brown, a human, tall and erect. At his left shoulder a wide, looping gold chain clashed dimly with his movements. He stopped when she raised her hand.

"Please don't come any closer, Andor."

He bowed his head slightly, and his long chestnut hair caught and held Yamth's light. "Is he hurt?" he asked,

"No, I don't think so." She stood up, walked over to him in her long stride.

"I won't go near him," he said, as she positioned herself between him and the figure on the ground.

"This is illusion, Andor, and I don't want to come out of it to find we've . . . I've done some terrible injury to him."

He bowed his head again, folded his arms across his chest in another random glitter of sound, like wind chimes. "Have you thought about the injury you've already done?"

Her head came up.

"He called you Chaeya."

"I know."

"That's a dangerous attachment he's formed."

"Yes. I didn't realize it before, although the signs must have been there . . . a long time ago."

"He has obligations, a duty to his people—"

"Don't you think I know that? Are you my conscience this time, Andor?"

"As you said, I'm an illusion." There was mockery there, sliding through the words spoken in the rich nasal undertones of the Ronadjounian language.

She glanced away toward M'landan. "I could leave—go somewhere else—"

"If you go now, while he's still asleep."

She looked back at the man—high ambassador, lord, leader of an alliance of worlds. "No. His seizures may not be over. And his eyes won't close . . . the sun. . . ."

"Leave when he wakes, then."

He moved his body slightly, and she caught the faint, fresh scent from him that penetrated the cloud of honey fragrance rising from her hands. "You've seen his conflict, and he's told you about the suspicion his people have of you. He won't be able to handle it, Areia."

"I know. I'll go when he wakens."

"Go far from here, where there'll be no accidental meetings. You have to make him understand you won't see him again."

She turned away from him, putting her hands on her hips—an old mannerism—and felt the supple Artactan leather of her holster belt. She looked down at the bronze uniform, the gleaming Artactan boots, the pattern gun in its holster. And then she was viewing herself from outside, seeing herself standing with all the authority and arrogance of command that had been so natural to her, standing feet slightly apart, hands resting on her holster belt, head bent slightly within the silver helmet with its flaring copper emblem.

And now, outside that imposing figure, this self in M'dian robes, this deformity of that other self, said, "All my life I've been feared and hated and no one was ever aware of my fear, except that alien being who gave in compassion what another creature demanded in pain and fear. And now, because I continue to live—and God knows why I do—the bonds with his people are threatened. I didn't mean to cause this; it hasn't been deliberate—"

"But that's the result. Repay his kindness the only way you can, and leave."

"Yes, I'll leave." She looked toward the other self who still stood in quiet concentration an arm's length away. "I want to die, Andor, and I can't."

"The answer may be simple."

"If you know what it is, tell me. I'll reverse whatever mechanism it is that's repressing Life'send."

"I don't have the answer; perhaps he does."

The figure still lay quietly on the ground, breathing slowly, his hands lifting and falling with the rhythm.

"Look at his hands, Areia; his hands."

She saw their finely-textured skin, with its suggestion of iridescence, in sudden close resolution superimposed over his form, the long, slim fingers and the palms with their three concentric rings held like a message before her eyes.

She swung her head around to find both the figure and the man gone. All about her, the island grass moved in slow reaches and falls as the breeze played through it, leaving it sighing against the stalks of L'M'dia.

Reality now, a return of pain. She went back to M'landan's side and adjusted the hood over the shifted light from the white sun. She sat there while the bars of golden shadow swept across the deeper stationary shadows of Yamth, this apparent motion of white Baandla, time visible.

And so it must be in his hands. In this violent liquid of his body that anointed the rituals and beliefs and all the ceremonies, this sacred laanva of the priest's hands misused to relieve her pain. This was the repressant of Life'send. But in violating whatever religious ethic that was involved in their hand contact he suffered not only mental anguish, but physical pain as well that threatened his life. And she would not allow that again.

She adjusted the hood again, and the soft purple band folded inward to the corner of his mouth. She stared at it, at the long curling upper lip and the soft broad lower lip that stretched in the wide whimsical line across his face.

Ah, M'landan, you called me Chaeya. . . .

In the distance she now began to hear the shifts of melody that were M'dian conversation, light trills and repetitions that danced back and forth over the islands like butterflies. She leaned forward. "M'landan." And more urgently, "M'landan!" He stirred, closed the lids of his eyes.

"M'landan!" she said again, shaking him gently. "Can you hear me?"

He opened his eyes then, and she knew immediately that he was fully conscious.

"The harvesters are coming," she told him, and he sat up, looked about him, saw the marks of his struggle, realized she had been with him.

"You shouldn't have followed me," he said reproachfully, severely.

"You shouldn't have tried to keep this from me," she replied with equal severity.

There was a short trill close at hand. M'landan rose unsteadily to his feet and might have fallen, but she had come up beside him and braced his weight.

"Will you be all right?"

"Yes. It takes a moment." Gradually he shifted away from her until he was standing unaided. "Thank you. My strength is coming back now."

He looked over his shoulder. Her eyes followed his glance, catching his anxiety, suddenly sharing his guilt.

"I'll go back to my camp," she said.

He hesitated, unsure, reluctant, trying to think clearly. "You'll come back to the city by fourth sunfall?"

Twenty-six hours. "Maybe." Her resolution? She had made it to Andor Seldoldon, but he was an illusion and M'landan was real, his anxiety palpable. Still, "I'll come back," was all the commitment she made.

But hours of hallucination followed, bitter, wrenching plots and scenarios that sprang from the deep well of her experience. She fell through burning worlds that tore the air from her lungs and left her searing on ashes, hurtled down waterways that dropped for miles and trapped her drowning in turbulence so deep it scored the center of all time.

And between hallucinations she lay on the green M'dian sand, staring up through the thin atmospheric shadow at the stars, considering what she was doing to the being who was her friend.

Chapter 3

It was long after *tlee haaranu* that she finally made her slow way back to the haruund and her own room, where she slept for over four sunfalls, undisturbed, waking now and again to go to the bathroom, to drink water from the silver faucet, then return across the soft thick floor to the ledge and sleep.

When she finally came around, she was cautious in her contact with the M'dians. Almost all of their work, which included their weaving, their silver work—the planet had an abundance of that metal exuded from rocky crevices in millennia past in its pure form—the myriad processes that involved L'M'dia, whether fiber, food, or oil, all took place in the haruund.

When she had realized Life'send had been delayed, she had convinced M'landan that she would at least feel useful if she could participate in some part of the community's life.

"What is it you would like to do?" he had asked her as they sat in the gathering room near one of the window openings.

She had answered thoughtfully, "Some jobs would be too dangerous for me, which is the only reason I'm not considering them, processing the aldaam for instance. I might accidentally ingest some. Or refining the oil—the way it's absorbed by the skin. . . ." She shook her head. "I don't think I'd better risk it. The same applies to the weaving and garment-making. But I think there is one place I could be useful—the laundry."

"The klaamet?" he said with a quaver of surprise and something else. Then he said, "There is the silver shop."

She smiled at him. "That requires skill and artistry, which I can appreciate, but which, unfortunately, are not among my talents."

27

"Tlaima could teach you."

"Tlaima is an artist, M'landan. What an ordeal for an artist to be obligated to a student who is hopelessly lacking in even a small talent. No, I think the laundry would be the best place for me."

"And there is structure repair—"

"Yes. And if I were to hallucinate about the time I reached the top of a ladder with a hammer in my hand, I'd drop it on someone's head. No, I think it would be safest for me and everyone else if I were to work in the laundry." Then she laughed, because he was so obviously discomfited by the thought.

"Even the ex-captain of a space ship can wash clothes, M'landan—" there was a quick downward twist to her smile "—if she's shown how."

"I don't know," he replied in a rare comeback, "some things are too difficult for even the most accomplished people."

Her sudden laugh brought heads around to look at her and at M'landan, who was folding his hands demurely into his sleeves, his eyes sparkling.

So she had gone to work in the klaamet for a few hours each day, gathering up the robes of the community and plunging them into the great low tubs and from there into the clear water, then through the presses and onto the drying racks that were arranged around the grassy courtyard of the klaamet. The washing room was a large, high, airy space that the breeze flowed through, and it reminded Darenga of summer on Earth, although the association was vague and she had never analyzed it. But she enjoyed this labor and the people she shared it with, two M'dians in particular—Sklova, a female, and Braunsi, a rather shy and clumsy male. They were amazed by her strength, the ease with which she handled the heavier chores of the klaamet. Darenga found a certain satisfaction in this; it seemed, in a strange way, a reaffirmation of what she had been. So she lifted and carried, scrubbed and flung robes onto drying racks, rejoicing in the smooth and disciplined movements of her body, the fineness of its response, rejoicing that the mastery and control were still there, even with so humble a task as this, and she looked forward to each day with pleasure.

Regularly, Tlaima brought M'landan's robes to the klaamet, but no one handled them but her. The tubs that were used were filled afresh. Darenga participated in this, at least, and then stood watching as Tlaima washed and rinsed the purple-banded robes and laid them carefully on a special rack to dry in the ruddy combined light of Yamth and Baandla.

Afterward each tub was emptied, and Darenga learned that the reason for all this special care was the cleansing away and dispersal back to the elements of any sacred laanva that might have accidentally spilled from his hands. This was all taken very seriously by everyone, and Darenga had tempered her first amused response and began to feel a subtle change in her own attitude about the robes. Certainly, when his garments were brought into the klaamet, his presence was there as well.

The M'dians she worked with had become accustomed to her short spells of hallucination, which usually took the form of a trance that lasted a few minutes, no more than five. And they would simply walk around her or lead her to the side of the room where she would remain until she came out of it.

But one late second sunfall, she turned from a rinsing tub to see a soldier of the Solar force swing through the doorway of the klaamet, his rifle held ready at his waist. As she yelled, "Get down! Get down!" her pattern gun was already in her hand, and she was spinning the dials and adjusting the pressure bars even as she knew the bone-white armor he wore was protection against the frequencies aimed against him.

He swept the rifle around, burning the tub behind her as she dove, sliding on the wet floor and twisting up against a second tub into a crouch. She jammed her side weapon back into the holster, spread her fingers up to the edge of the tub and braced the toe of her boot against the bottom staves. She could hear his breathing as he moved out into the room.

"Where's Lord Andor's lady captain?" he sneered in harsh Arcustan, and, having him solidly placed, Darenga shoved forward, overturning the tub and flooding the water toward him in a sheet.

"Here, you Arcus son-of-a-bitch!" she yelled, leaping around the rolling tub and through the water as he brought the rifle up. The laser burned into her side, and she screamed in pain and rage as her body collided with his and they went down in a heap on the wet floor. His rifle flew out of his hands, skittered against the far wall. She had her knee into his throat between the heavy slickness of his helmet and body armor, but he flung her off and they both came up clawing for a hold and fell back against a tub of soapy water.

"Seldoldon's mother-whore," he wheezed, and she could see the red smear of his eyes through the helmet slit as her hands caught his throat and they pitched sideways into the water.

She rolled under him as he clubbed at her with his forearms, coming up through the alkaline sting of the suds blinding her, groping, then finding the thick neck that lay under the armor. She held him down, grating out Arcustan obscenities to the image beneath the water, her mind screaming, "Die, you bastard! Drown—it's the only clean thing you'll ever do!"

And then she rose up out of the soap and water and drifting foam, her hands clutched around who knew whose robe, her own robe wrung heavily to her body, her hair clinging to the sides of her face and drooling with suds. She stared around at her co-workers, who had taken refuge against the walls and who now stood staring at her in astonishment.

She saw herself then, no uniform, no holster belt with weapon, no enemy's throat in her frozen grip. She let the robe fall back into the water and, pulling together as much dignity as she found left in her, started to get out of the tub. There was a sudden high shimmering sound of M'dian laughter along the walls, and then Braunsi came forward and held out his hands to help her.

"Captain," he said, "I congratulate your victory. Playmo's robe is truly a fierce opponent." He said it so solemnly she dissolved instantly to laughter so hard she had to hold the sides of the tub to stay upright.

They were all a little more watchful of her after that, but their attitude was sympathetic. Certainly they understood the very real danger she represented, but they accepted her nevertheless, in the generous and tolerant way of the M'dian people.

News traveled fast both into and out of the klaamet, and

it wasn't many hours before M'landan must have heard the tale, because Braunsi came up to her not long after looking sheepish and ill-at-ease.

"I have an apology to make, Captain," he gave as preamble.

"Apology? For what?"

"For having laughed at you. *Mlo saindla;* that was unkind of me. You cannot help these dreams you have."

"Mmm," she replied. "I detect a priestly hand in this."

"My thoughtlessness was explained to me," he answered noncommittally.

She stared at him for a long moment. "I accept your apology," she said finally, not wanting to undermine M'landan's discipline. "But it was funny, wasn't it?" She grinned at him.

His mouth broadened. "Yes, Captain," he answered. "I'll have to admit it surely was, once it was over. Playmo's poor robe. . . ."

M'landan never mentioned hearing about the incident to her, and it occurred to her then that the associated guilt he felt was too strong and deep for him to bring the subject up.

Although all the community activities were carried on in the haruund, no one lived there but her and M'landan—he in his separate cell that no one was permitted to enter, she in a room far down a distant corridor. All the citizens of Ilanu lived, as each generation always lived, in dormitory-like facilities scattered around the city. When mates were chosen they would select the individual dwellings, the single domes which would be their home, where they would have the two children—male and female—which each female would bear at the age of seventy. And ten years after that all this generation would be dead, and only the children would remain to tend the plants and carry on the customs of their species. A strange and violent symbiosis.

Darenga hadn't seen M'landan since she had returned, except in the gathering room, briefly, no conversation, eye contact at fifteen yards, and once in the corridor where he would have stopped, she was certain, but someone came along and he merely gestured, moving past her in a subtle wave of honey fragrance.

But there were frequent religious observances, and she inadvertently came on one outside the complex one day.

31

The context of it involved some aspect of L'M'dia, which such observances usually did, and she was not able to grasp the ritual's full significance, but M'landan commanded its center, his dramatic baritone guiding the voices of the crowd, eliciting responses that rose from the collective instinct he triggered. She felt the reverence, the deep belief that moved the crowd under his guidance. Klayon and Tlaima assisted him, knowing their roles in this ritual, performing them with respect. Their place in this society was assured, their lives secure.

Darenga watched the ceremony to its conclusion, standing at the fringes of the crowd, not knowing the responses, not joining in the songs. When she saw M'landan moving with two or three of the people into the city, she left.

The hallucinations continued, diminishing gradually until they were sporadic and infrequent. And with the decreasing hallucinations came an increase in pain; the early sign of Life'send. The concentration required for her to keep it under control, to keep it from dominating her, was exhausting.

It was becoming obvious that M'landan was avoiding her, and, after thoughtful consideration, her assessment was that it was time for her to leave. Now that the earlier friction she had generated had subsided, it was time to leave still a welcome guest.

Once, a long time ago, she had gone to M'landan's quarters, but, having learned after that of the code she had violated, she had never gone again. Nevertheless, she believed she owed him the courtesy of telling him she was leaving, and it was this reason that finally brought her to the gathering room again.

It was after second sunfall, the dinner hour, and groups of M'dians still remained in the hall, quietly talking, most of them sipping hanj, the fermented liquid of the L'M'dia bud. It was a social drink with broad associations of friendship and good humor. No M'dian in all the years she had been in contact with the planet had ever drunk to intoxication, although some of the humans stationed on that planet had quickly abused the drink.

She entered through the screens and stood to one side, surveying the room for M'landan, but he wasn't there. Since it was his habit to come in at some time during this period, she sat down on the ledge near one of the window openings to wait for him, and turned to look out over the plain.

"Areia?"

She recognized the sad-sweet voice before she looked up to see the female standing before her. "Hello, Tlaima. Sit down with me."

"I haven't seen you for a while," Tlaima said softly.

"I was in the Yarbeen. And my hours in the klaamet have changed."

"Are you waiting for M'landan?"

"I was hoping to catch him, yes."

"I saw him speaking with some of the weavers. He should be here soon."

"Thank you. I think I'll wait, then."

Tlaima sat looking at her with her enormous black eyes. Like the features of all the M'dians, her nose was broad, sweeping into the upper lip, but the curve of her mouth was soft, turned slightly down at the corners, which gave her a kindly expression. Her skin, smooth-textured and without visible pores, as all her species, had, by some genetic combination, a fully iridescent quality, the light glancing from it in a rainbow sheen with every movement.

Darenga, never very artful at the small talk of any beings, sat thinking that when M'landan made his choice it should be this lovely, gentle, and perceptive female.

But he had called her Chaeya. *I'm out of place,* she thought. *Out of sequence, out of time; overlived and overspent.*

She stood up. "When M'landan comes in—" she began, and then saw danger, like a warning light, approaching.

"May we join you, Tlaima?" Laatam—confident, deliberate, aggressive within the boundaries of the M'dian personality.

Trolon, her right arm, came up beside her, and behind him, Samar and Quanti: the Greynin, informally gathered.

Tlaima seemed to sense what had been immediately apparent to Darenga, trained from birth in the parrying of aggressive behavior. "Need a sister ask if she is welcome?" said Tlaima, and Darenga made a swift reappraisal of that gentle M'dian, realizing she had been allowing superficial impressions to guide her assessments of the individual—a dangerous practice—and she wondered that she had not recognized this in Tlaima before.

"Captain Darenga," said Laatam, "sit down please."

The arrangement of the group prevented Darenga's movement forward, and she sat down slowly, all the old instincts suddenly alive.

But it seemed so natural, the addition of that group to their number, and friendly.

The preliminaries of all conversations on all worlds that she had ever been in contact with went on, and Darenga responded as was required, gauging all the while the direction.

"Captain Darenga," Quanti said politely, "I saw you at *Draad;* you don't attend many of our religious festivals."

Darenga sat with her hands folded over her crossed knees. "No," she replied, "there is a great deal about your religion I don't understand." That was true, and the truth of the statement rang in her voice.

"But our priest, surely, has explained much of it to you; he has been your companion for many years now." This was Trolon.

Darenga looked over at him where he sat on the ledge beyond Tlaima and Laatam. "He's explained those points of it I've asked about. But friends talk about many subjects over the years."

"Yes. Everyone, I suppose, is curious to learn about the places you have been, the worlds you have seen."

Laatam, Darenga thought, *do you realize who you are dealing with?*

"And you?" she asked quietly. "What would you like to know?"

"We've been told by the humans who were here," put in Samar, "that there was a great passageway through the stars from our world to yours."

"Yes," Darenga replied, "there was." No elaboration.

"Like a street?" This was from one of the M'dians who were unobtrusively gathering about her, as they eventually did whenever she came into the room.

"No, like the corridors in this building."

"And you can see it?" someone else asked.

"Not exactly, if you mean can your eyes perceive it, no. There are instruments that detect it, and mathematical equations are derived from the information the instruments give. A . . ." she searched for an analogy ". . . picture is formed, a map that describes the configuration. . . ." It was beyond their understanding. They were an intelligent, curious people by nature, but their experience was too limited, their preparation too slight.

"You have seen many wonderful things," said Laatam, "things that you have told us about before. Tell us again about Yamth and Baandla."

You're playing a reckless game with me, Darenga thought grimly. "What is there for me to tell? All M'dians who open their eyes can see what they are." Nothing in the melody to reveal deception, but the truth she spoke was taken in another meaning by Laatam.

"Perhaps some have not opened their eyes," she said, and Darenga granted her the control that permitted no discordancy in *her* song.

"Someone in Klada?" Darenga replied neutrally.

There was a little shimmer through the listeners.

"Even in Klada, people know the gods," Trolon said.

"Then the gods are recognized everywhere on M'dia," she replied.

"And you, Captain," Laatam put in smoothly, "do you recognize our gods?"

She had not seen M'landan enter, but all of a sudden there he was, standing within the crowd at Samar's shoulder, his hood thrown back, his eyes brilliant. "Whose belief do you question, Laatam?" he said mildly. But there was no doubt that she had committed a grave breach of etiquette, and M'landan had made the people listening acutely aware of it.

Darenga tried to catch his eye. *Be careful, M'landan; she will not be easily defeated.*

"I question no one's beliefs, my priest," Laatam answered. "It is doubt I am concerned with."

"Does anyone here doubt the gods?" he asked the company in a sonorous tone.

Of course no one did.

"The captain has not spoken," said Samar.

M'landan turned his great, bright eyes on him. "Samar, are you trying to make a mystery?"

Darenga had never heard this tone from him, didn't know it existed in the M'dian expression; a slightly derisive note, the subtle expression of a superior male.

And Samar, no match for this confrontation, was silent.

M'landan addressed the people around him. "Samar

considers the face of things and forgets the force that directs us all. Sai Yamth and Sai Baandla trace their paths above, while we run below at random, unprepared, given to the counsel of our own desires when our eyes should be following the guidance of their light. Our gods do not move from their paths because one among us seems not to believe."

He was drawing attention away from Laatam's part in this, she realized, and wondered why.

"Neither should we be moved, but show the loving patience that has always guided us, knowing that faith comes from example as well as exhortation."

And how do you reconcile Samar, eloquent priest? Now that Laatam and I both have been so adroitly covered?

"Samar is my brother," he said then, using the phrase that meant brother of the flesh, rather than the broader term with the connotation of an association through mutual ideas and interests. It had an effect on the listeners as well as on Samar, who placed his hands in his sleeves and bowed his head.

How many of these responses are genetically arranged? How much of it is M'landan's skill and the force of his personality? We were here so long and learned so little about them.

Darenga watched M'landan cup his long hand over Samar's ear membrane, and, having experienced the strange effect of that hand, knew Samar would be mollified. But now M'landan cupped his other hand to Samar's head, and she was aware that when he spoke Samar would be receiving an overlay of vibrations in an organ so sensitive the human ear seemed primitive in comparison, and at this calming technique M'landan was the undisputed master.

"A brother may be rebuked but still remain at the heart's center."

A wave of forgiveness ran through the group around Samar and M'landan. More than a sympathetic response generated by the mood, it was a direct effect of the infinitely complex series of frequencies that were far out of reach of the human ear. So Darenga understood from the subtle movements and eye expressions of the M'dians in the room what she actually could not hear.

Now M'landan stepped back, slipped his hands into his

sleeves. "My brother," he said to Samar then, "I have a message I would have you deliver."

The change in the atmosphere was immediate. A suppressed excitment in the room now. Darenga perceived the change, but hardly knew the reason.

"I will deliver it, my priest," Samar answered formally.

By reactions around her, Darenga sensed that this was an honor bestowed on Samar, a quick shift of emotions and events for him from rebuke to esteem. Darenga saw the swift manipulation in this, but had no idea of its ultimate purpose.

Samar and M'landan walked slowly away toward the doorway, everyone in the room intent on them. They stopped near the screens, a perfect backdrop for the two figures robed in gold, a backdrop of rich brown and deep emerald hazed with purple, the color repeated in the soft purple band of M'landan's hood, making him the central figure in the tableau.

And this is theatrical, Darenga said to herself as she sat watching him make his slow turn to face both Samar and the audience. *He has a flair for it, and he does it so well. They're all caught up by him.* She glanced around.

Tlaima, next to her, sat erect, her head toward the door, a rainbow down the side of her face where the light struck it at just the right angle. Her hands lay upturned in her lap, one inside the other, the palm rings in the one just visible in the curve of her hand. Beyond her, Laatam sat in an identical pose, and beyond her, Trolon, standing with his body facing Laatam, but his head toward the figures at the doorway.

"Say what message you would have me give," Samar entoned.

A message of ritual and form, one whose contents everyone seemed to anticipate. A message that would be said aloud for the audience and to the one to whom it would be addressed through Samar. Darenga sat wondering at the purpose for this display coming so close on the heels of confrontation.

"You must say for me what I cannot say for myself, Samar, for when I try to speak my throat is dry, and there is no sound."

It was a complaint that was common, Darenga gathered from the responses around her.

"My eyes grow bright on one image that moves before my path."

The problems of a lover? Instantly, she realized that that was exactly what he was describing. He was going to pick the Chaeya. And suddenly she wanted to leave, and would have quietly found a way out if she could have done so unobtrusively. She felt acutely an intruder, sensed it in the glances that fell on her from everyone in the room but M'landan, and, because it was his performance, his stage, his audience, they accepted that his ignoring her meant she was to remain, and their attention went back to him and did not shift again.

"Who is this one you would have me speak to?" Samar asked.

M'landan's answer began on a low minor note that set a vibration along the palms of Darenga's hands.

"She whose song I have heard in the stillness of my chamber at third sunfall. She whom I have seen walked clothed in the radiance of Yamth and Baandla when, as a child removed from other children, I watched her from my window as she moved among the islands. Her hands were pale against the buds. Her hands held the globe and the stalk. In her hands she held the perfect globe and it shone with a light that pierced my eyes, and my eyes would not be closed, nor would they shield against that light. My eyes have seen no other one since that time; her image lies across my vision; her name is sweet in my mouth. She is the one I have called Chaeya, my brother."

Darenga drew in a long, painful breath.

"Which of our sisters have you chosen?" said Samar. "Tell me, and I will ask for her acceptance."

There was a long pause, and Darenga, with all the intuition borne of years of rigid self-control, knew the reason for it.

"Laatam," M'landan said simply, directly.

Darenga felt a sudden movement and glanced to the side to see Tlaima's hands turn and her body go still. At the same time, she saw Laatam rise in a slow, stately motion and, before she obscured him, Trolon, rigid, his eyes the color of lead.

All this suppressed and sudden emotion swept around Darenga, struggling to bring her own feelings under control. The one thought that struck her clearly was that

Laatam had not for a single moment considered M'landan would make any other choice. Darenga heard her say, "Tell my brother, my priest, I accept the honor he has given me," in a calm tone.

"The honor is mine," M'landan replied, without waiting for Samar to pass her acceptance to him. With that, Laatam joined M'landan, Samar stepped aside, and the couple, now formally betrothed, went out through the screens.

There was a sudden rush of lilting, excited conversation through the room, a harsh unM'dian sound from Trolon, quickly stifled by a note from Samar, a trill from Quanti that meant Darenga had no idea what, and nothing from Tlaima at all. As for herself, there was no name she could give to her own feelings, if she had any; like a cymbal, she had been struck unwilling and she was still numb.

Chapter 4

For several sunfalls there had been talk of little else but the coming shoma. Darenga, completely in the dark about the customs surrounding the preparations, and hesitant to ask the M'dians anything on a subject they had always remained silent on, gleaned what she could from the conversations around her.

All gossip comes to the laundry was the M'dian saying, and there was truth enough in that. She learned that now that M'landan had made his choice, everyone else was free for shoma also. A joining of anyone but the priest was not particularly elaborate, hardly of the magnitude of the forthcoming ceremony which would—as M'landan had said—be performed by Klada's priest, most of that city coming with him. This event, she discovered, was the sole reason for the vast numbers of silent and empty rooms in the haruund. Once in every generation the rooms were filled.

But in the meantime, M'landan was busy performing shoma ceremonies for the lovers who had proclaimed early and had been waiting patiently for their priest to do the same. Most of the conversation in the klaamet was about who was pairing with whom, how long they had been waiting; switches that were being made now that the moment of decision had arrived, and all the other embroilments of courtship that Darenga was astounded to find had been going on all the time she'd been on the planet. She could only conclude they were not a publicly affectionate people. But then, none of the research teams trained in that sort of probing had found anything more about the M'dian sex life than that the priest of one generation fathered the priest for the next.

She had postponed her leave-taking because it hardly seemed an appropriate time to bring it up to M'landan. Yet now it had been some time since the announcement of the shoma, and still she seldom saw M'landan because of the activities. When she did, Laatam was always by his side.

But she wanted to be gone, far away from the city into the shadow of the Yarbeen, before this joining that she had no desire now to see, to become accustomed to a solitary life as Life'send progressed. She was determined now to remove herself from M'landan's compassionate concern for her.

She didn't know if M'landan had been staying in the haruund; she would not go near his room, although she often paced the corridors of the building in the silence of third and fourth sunfalls. Now she actively sought him out, found him standing with a group just outside the haruund, Laatam at his side. Not far away stood Trolon, the queen's guard.

Darenga came up to them, and in her politest M'dian, said, "M'landan, may I speak with you?"

He excused himself to Laatam, to the group, and they moved off to one side, out of range of even those sensitive ears.

"I'm leaving at third sunfall, M'landan." Her tone was soft, and held more regret than she intended. "You've been very kind to me, my friend—"

He interrupted in a voice that hadn't been used on her since she'd left the Maintainer Academy. "I will speak with you about this later," and he turned abruptly away and went back to the waiting group.

"You will?" she echoed in shock and sudden anger. She swung around in a little burst of sand. *Oh you will?* she said again to herself, and went back into the complex.

She felt like a great burning fool, and if the decision to leave had been difficult for her to make before, the carrying out of it would be simple. She had hung around on the strength of what she had perceived to be his outpouring of feeling for her, reluctant—at least be honest!—*dreading* to leave him. And all the while his embarrassment had been growing, and she cursed herself in Arcustan, that mother curse language of them all, cursed and railed against her stupidity and foolishness.

Darenga said her farewells to Sklova and Braunsi, in the next sunfall, and sought Tlaima out in her quarters to say goodbye.

"Does M'landan know you are leaving?"

"Yes." A hard tone. Tlaima's eyes rested, a heavy question, on her face.

"You might tell him when you see him that I left still his friend."

"I will tell him."

"Goodbye, Tlaima," she said, laying her hand briefly on her shoulder.

"Yamth and Baandla guide your path," Tlaima replied.

"Thank you," Darenga said, after a pause, then swung around and crossed the silent room to the door.

It was third sunfall, and Ilanu lay sleeping under the red light of Yamth and the quick swerving shadow play of Baandla. The haruund was deserted, everyone gone home, all work finished until first sunfall. Darenga stood at the door of her room, her cloak thrown about her shoulders. In one long fold pocket of her robe was a small packet of dried raspberry root, and hanging from her shoulder a bottle of water, these provisions to get her the twenty kilometers to the Yarbeen and her old camp, where she planned to rest before continuing in a direction she had yet to choose. But that was all she was taking. Nothing more. She took a last glance then turned away into the corridor.

She had not gone very far when she encountered M'landan coming swiftly along, his robes filling the passage like great downswept wings.

"What are you doing!" He came to a swirling stop and turned his enormous stare down on her.

"I told you I was leaving," she said calmly.

"I said I would talk to you later."

"Yes, you did."

"You weren't going to wait!"

"I've been waiting for about one hundred sunfalls; I couldn't wait any longer."

He stood analyzing the quality of her voice, the timbre and pitch, all the meaning he could suck from her statement. "*Mlo saindla*," he said finally, "but you surprised me. I couldn't understand why you would want to go *now*."

It was her turn to show surprise. She shook her head, smiled without humor. "You've confused me. I would think especially now."

He was still breathing heavily from his long run up

through the corridors, and he waited the space of several breaths before he replied, "Since Laatam will be the Chaeya now, she is no longer in the Greynin. A new member will be chosen, and there will be a new composition and a new direction, I think." He paused again. "Her obligations to her mate and priest will keep her silent." That was certainly straightforward.

"Why did you do a thing like that!" she cried, her voice heavy with distress.

"Because I knew what you were going to answer to her challenge, and I would have had to cast you out of the city the moment you said it."

"I . . . didn't know," she said stupidly. And then stiffly, "It wasn't necessary. You didn't have to do it. It wouldn't have mattered anyway."

"Why do you say it doesn't matter?" Too many conflicting emotions in her ragged song; he couldn't separate them.

"Of course it matters; I didn't mean that. But you shouldn't have done it. I'm going to leave anyway."

"There is no *need* for you to go. There is no circumstance now that would demand you leave this city. You are still under my protection; there is no one here who will question that again."

She shook her head, made a wild agitated circle with her hand, trying to free herself from what she heard in his voice. "I can't, I can't," she said. "I can't. I'm going. Let me pass."

"Wait! Talk with me first. If you must go, I will not try and stop you. But let's not part this way . . . in this turmoil."

When she halted her movement forward, he dropped his voice, softened the melody, but the effort was audible. "We have always tried to understand each other, isn't that so?"

"I think we have."

"I will try to understand this . . . why you would want to leave me."

"Leave you!"

"Come," he said then, turning, slipping his hands into his sleeves, calm now. "There are better places to talk than this hallway."

He started up the corridor, and she followed him as he glided noiselessly ahead of her.

Living with the M'dians had made her conscious of sound in a way she had never been before, and she had learned to be aware of noises she had previously filtered out. There were the grosser sounds like breathing, movements, footsteps, and the slighter noises that drew their own picture of the environment—those she had learned to hear. But the M'dians could hear the rustle of cloth from a heartbeat, and with the acutest sense of hearing of all was M'landan, who could identify any of his people by the sound of the inner membrane of their eyes. It was another dimension, an overlay of sound composite on the visual. She could only imagine what the actual world of a M'dian was like.

M'landan was stepping through a doorway, and she came to a halt just outside where he stood half-turned in the entrance of the screen-maze.

"I won't go in there, M'landan, I told you that," she said, and started to turn away from his chamber.

"Chaeya," he replied softly, "you have been in this room from the moment you came through these screens in ignorance of our customs, in pain and fear, asking me for help. You have never left it."

So solemn, so loving. After a moment, she said, "And if someone should come?"

"No one will come. But if they should, they would not enter."

He stood quietly until she finally moved forward, and then he turned and led her through the screens.

It was as she remembered it, a glowing shell of pale gold, the ledge rich in softly designed cushions and mattings, softly colored cloths of stylized L'M'dia. The floor fiber was thick, soundless. The window was swung wide to the plain and the steady light of Yamth and the swift undulation of Baandla. And, as if it breathed from the walls, the faint odor of honey.

M'landan crossed silently to the window, closed it, and the room took on a quiet afternoon glow.

"Do you think that will shut out your gods, M'landan?"

"No. But it may dim the sound of our voices to anyone passing nearby."

"I'm sorry," she said. "That was foul; I shouldn't have said it."

"I understand."

She looked away from his calm gaze. "You've made just about every compromise for me you can." Her eyes came back to his face. "The conflict—"

"There is no conflict now. Everything is in agreement."

"And there's no conflict in you? You're going into shoma with Laatam and call me Chaeya?"

"I do no one dishonor. Laatam will be my mate, and esteemed for it. There will be no more dissension. I've not done anything dishonorable. And you can stay in the haruund in peace—" he had started to raise his hand, and she drew back. "If you would keep me away, tell me not to touch you."

Silence.

He put his hand back into his sleeve, turned quietly, and went to the ledge and sat down. His eyes were on her, no reflection.

"I don't mean to sound unkind—" she began.

"You don't sound unkind. I hear what you think you hide from me. You have a great arrogance, Chaeya; you think me innocent in all things and yourself responsible."

"Don't try to manipulate me—"

"Honesty is not manipulation. If I wanted to manipulate you—" a quick decrescendo, a phrase, so brief, notes only of terrible sadness, no words. Darenga felt the tears well up hot against her eyelids, the sadness, not projected into her but rising from the buried griefs inside her. "You are the only one I am freed from trying to manipulate," he said, watching her pull her hand across her eyes, "and although I can, I don't want to. I've never wanted to."

"Don't ever . . . don't ever do that to me again!" she told him, realizing as she said it that she sounded on the verge of hysteria. She took a deep breath, but everything was thin, drawn tight.

"I won't," he said. "Why do you want to leave?"

"Why in the world do you want me to stay!"

"Haven't I answered that question?"

"I don't know," she replied. "This isn't getting us anywhere." Still that note of hysteria threatening to slide up into some freakish scream all out of proportion and distorted from what she really felt or meant or was. This clash of emotion and conditioning, this utterance against time, swift and fluid, this compulsion of honor and obligation. Only she wasn't a Maintainer anymore, and there was

45

nothing for her to maintain but a wretched body and a sinking mind.

Time to go, to leave, to have done.

"Let me comfort you," he said.

"You can't."

"Let me try."

"I'm locked into what I am." That was no explanation.

"Tell me what your conflict is, and I will resolve it." The priest speaking now. "I will give you absolution."

There was a bitter edge to her sudden laugh. "I've seen your gods, M'landan. I've measured their radiation. Yamth is 2500°c. at its surface, and Baandla 8000°c.—too hot for me to embrace."

"Then embrace me. Believe in me. I am your loving friend who has never wished you any harm."

"I know that."

"Then let me help you."

"There's nothing you can do. It's inside me. Something done a long time ago."

He leaned back against the wall then, his eyes on her face. "We have led lives in parallel, Areia; you on your Earth, me on this planet. We were conceived to serve our people and trained from childhood in how to perform that service. You were taught how to protect, to reward, to punish, to see that everything was kept stable for the lives of those under your care. And so it was with me. And here lies your conflict . . . as well as my own."

Astute, thoughtful, to the core of the problem. She remained motionless, listening.

"I said you think me innocent in all things and yourself guilty—of self-indulgence, I would imagine, and of not adhering to your responsibilities to beings who depend on you. And I said that was arrogant of you to take the blame for the misery and guilt you've seen in me when it was a situation of my own making."

"But that's where you're wrong! I made demands on you—"

"That's true. And there was a great struggle in me when you came to this room—but you know that. Let me ask you about that first time in the Yarbeen so many years ago when I took your hands—" there was a slight blur in his tone "—what did you think then?"

"I . . . I knew you had just received your bands making

you priest. You offered some kind of benediction because I was leaving, and we had been friends. You invoked your gods and said, 'Let this one who far-journeys find peace!' "

"Ah, you remember."

"Yes, I remember."

"And what of this third, most recent, time?"

"You felt compassion for me because you knew I was experiencing pain again." She looked away from him.

"And, Chaeya," he demanded softly, "tell me what your thoughts were when you touched my face and drew me down beside you."

She still didn't look at him, but instead answered harshly, "Our research teams explained our physiology and mating patterns to you." Against her will, there was a flare of remembered sensation. "I don't understand the purpose of this—"

"And what do you know of our physiology and mating patterns?"

"Nothing, as you well know, except you lack the sex organs—" she almost said *I need*, "—of human males."

He looked at her for a moment, evaluating the savage undertone. "You strike out because showing me your need makes you feel vulnerable. Are we not friends? Didn't we agree on that?"

"Yes, of course we're friends, but—"

"No reservations; we have declared ourselves friends, and friends do not harm each other. Isn't that so?"

"We're friends."

"Come here, my friend, I want to show you something about me."

"M'landan—"

"Please. I indicated I would not touch you, and I will not. Please come here; stand here in front of me."

When she had complied, he drew his hands from his sleeves, slowly, so as not to make her uneasy, for he perceived in the position of her body the tension that would send her lurching away from him instantly if he moved to touch her.

He lay his hands on his knees palms up and said, "Tell me what you know about my hands."

She stared down at the soft skin, the circle within a circle within a circle. Somewhere inside the tight scaffolding of her ribs a signal rose to her brain and was vocalized in her head. *Look at you disintegrating. The molecules are flying off in streams. What are you going to do? . . . What are you going to do? . . . What are you going to do?*

She said stiffly, "You can produce laanva, which has certain religious uses—"

"Yes, and the laanva alters slightly according to the particular purpose that is being served. Did you know that?"

She hadn't known that. She had assumed the fluid remained the same.

"What else do you know, my friend?" A gentle, encouraging phrase. Where had she heard him use it before? The memory came swiftly. She had said to him, *I'm going to put my hand on you, if you don't object.*

An official laying on of hands, as commander of the M'dian mission in those brief days of madness before the war. She was performing this act to determine if he was using some Corrolean-type of mind projection—determining whether he existed or not. What idiocy! And he had answered her in just that same encouraging tone, *No I do not object.*

But she had not touched him, had instead sat staring out over the islands, her hands on the steering wheel of the roller sledge they were returning to Ilanu in from the Yarbeen. And he had asked, *Do you hesitate because I am alien to you?* When she hadn't answered, he had said, *Is touching important to you? Is it something you must do because we are friends? Is it your custom?* And they had finally clasped wrists, Maintainer fashion.

I have never touched anyone not of my people before, he had trilled excitedly. And they had sat joined, the M'dian child and the captain of the great Galaxy ship that circled his world, and even then the long slender fingers that lightly held her wrist had disquieted her.

"What else do you know?" he repeated.

What else? Could she talk about that "else" objectively? Dryly, as it had been given in one of the team reports?

L'M'dia is harvested in eighty-year cycles, the cycle being completed at the harvest period, when the elder generation severs the plant with large hinged knives at the base ring which is on each single stalk. In order to prevent irreparable damage to the stalk, the M'dian cutter must place his or her hand around the ring membrane. This causes the serum *laanva* to exude from the palm vents of the cutter, which then passes through the stalk membrane to combine with the ring fluid, immediately sealing the *aldaam*, or stalk fluids, in the stalk. When the *laanva* is passed through the ring membrane, the lethal toxin of the specialized ring fluid seeps back through the membrane and is absorbed by the palms of the harvesters, resulting in their death within hours after the harvest is completed. What the natural life span of the M'dian native would be is not known, although there have been suggestions that it could be as long as three hundred years.

Where had the tears come from? Not from that dry bit of information she had once read with a sense of curiosity on the Galaxy bridge. No tears then.

She wiped her eyes and found M'landan crying too, silently. "Chaeya, there's more in my hands than death," he told her.

"We didn't learn very much about you, M'landan . . . about your people. That's all I know."

"There is ease from pain," he said, controlled again.

"But it causes you pain."

"I accept it willingly."

"But I can't. Not when you could have blinded yourself or choked to death in the sand. . . ."

He leaned forward. "You haven't asked me why that happened."

That brought her up short. Why had it? Why that violent reaction? She looked at him.

He turned his eyes down on his hands as he slowly folded the palms together. "You lack the substance to neutralize my seed."

She started to speak, stared at him. ". . . My God!"

There were properties in that brief, hoarse utterance that he hadn't expected. A repugnance that edged on horror. It confused him, left him uncertain.

"My conflict," he went on slowly, "is because I am to be the father of the next generation, and my seed is limited." He stopped, still uncertain with only that brief twisted and truncated indication from her. "That is why a priest is

49

forbidden communion until *eretec*, the Time of Conception."

"But the other males . . . and shoma—they're all marrying."

"They are allowed communion throughout their lives because, although they produce the fluid, they have no seed. When they join with the one of their choice it is for the care of the children who follow from *eretec*. I am the father who continues my species, who has been given guardianship of the seed."

He turned his face up to her. "My seed is measured, but there is a reserve provided by the wisdom of the gods. Even in my passion, I have been cautious." His tone was circumspect; he had thought deeply and long on the consequences.

"I have come to an agreement between my obligations and my desire for you," he told her. "There has been nothing in all the history of my people, nothing in the Teachings, explaining how I should conduct myself in this case." He leaned back against the wall again, looking up at her from the shadow of his hood.

"Can you know how you appeared to us when, clothed in Yamth's light, your hair on fire, you came like Yamth descending from the sky? Everyone feared you—all of us, even my father. But it was a fear that came from awe. And you singled me out. Or was it I who dared approach you? No matter, the awe became something else. And I found much in us that was alike." The soft, encouraging tone again.

She had to respond. "I've thought the same many times."

"Yes! I'm sure you must have. It's obvious; I've often wondered why no one else saw it."

"Laatam and Trolon. . . ."

"Yes, they must have sensed something. But there is nothing now they can say, for the agreement I made with myself is this: my gods, Areia, are loving and forgiving. They are compassionate. They would not turn away from your pain, ignore you because you are alien, because you cannot tend L'M'dia. They shine equally on all living things that come into their light, and I find my answer in them. If what I do does not deprive my people or threaten their continuation—and I have assurances it does not—and if it eases your burden, then it is not wrong. I want you to stay here where I can care for you, where I know you are safe." He raised his hand but made no move to touch her. A gesture almost of benediction. "Ah, Areia, there have been so many years, so much we have said to each other . . . about worlds and time, about the great reaches beyond this lovely globe that is my planet, those things that you have seen, the thoughts that stir the minds of other sentient beings, and yet we've never talked like this."

"M'landan," she said, shaking free of his harmonics. "This is impossible. You're forbidden communion and you want me to—"

"It's true; the priest is forbidden communion. But when I considered the reasons such a restriction should exist, the answer I determined was that the restriction prevents indiscriminate waste of seed, a powerful temptation, I can assure you, although for me it was easier to abstain and follow my proper training than to succumb and lock hands with every female who caught my scent. Self-control, to be sustained, must be consistent." He lifted his hands back into his sleeves and leaned against the wall again. "In our communion, there isn't that difficulty. I . . . maintain restraint."

"And if your people were to discover this arrangement?"

"I am their priest. I will explain how it's within our laws."

He had that confidence; he radiated it, and she said carefully, because she felt his life depended on what she was going to say, "I've been on more worlds than you have ever known existed, M'landan. And I've seen more violence than you could ever imagine. And I know that when the survival of a species is threatened the members will respond with savagery and bloodshed no matter how tolerant they seem. If your people find out about this, they'll turn against you."

"I know my people," he replied.

"And you think you can control them because you've always been able to in the past. But that was a behavior mutually agreed upon. This is something very different."

It was finally coming back to her, the ability to reason, to judge, not to be distracted by his voice or the nearness of his body, where before she struggled in a morass of pain and emotion that had blurred her mind and distorted her judgment. "They wouldn't tolerate it, and I'm . . . under a moral obligation not to allow it. I *will* go, M'landan, because it's the only right thing to do—" and here she had to stop, for the notes that had begun to fall would dissolve the force and commitment in what had gone before.

He was looking at her with eyes that were obscured, silvered like the back of a mirror. She made a movement away and couldn't complete the turn. Slowly, his eyes cleared. "You cannot go," he said finally, perceiving.

"No," she answered. "Something in the laanva of your hands keeps me alive, and I can't refuse it." Her voice was bitter and twisted with the irony of the half-truth, for she had given him only part of the reason.

"It keeps you alive!" he echoed in a short melody so convoluted she couldn't understand it. He suddenly closed his eyes. "I feel your distress," he said. "I hold the wellspring of your life, and your distress is overpowering."

Now everything in his perception had shifted, and this broadened view drained a measure of his certainty away.

"Think clearly, M'landan; you have to see things as they are, the terrible potential for harm in the combination of Laatam and Trolon. She's ambitious and she's only realized part of that ambition. And Trolon is angry and resentful and controlled by her. She can exert a powerful influence, especially if—were they lovers?"

"Yes, I believe so."

"I thought as much when I saw Trolon's face that day in the gathering room. That makes it worse, of course. Recognize this danger and tell me to do what I can't do for myself; tell me to go, and I must obey." Her voice was urgent now, and he straightened forward to look up at her.

"I have seen the same events as you have. If I hadn't recognized the alliance of Laatam and Trolon, I would not have taken the measures I did. Perhaps it is as you say with Trolon's feelings now, for he does hang at a distance like a sentinel. I had dismissed it, because the priest's mate, once she has been selected, may have no other communion in her lifetime but at eretec, and if no other virtue rests in her, Laatam reveres form."

The confidence was flowing back into his voice now. He stood up. "There may still be uneasiness, but there is no danger. And it is as impossible for me to send you away as it is for you to go. I respect what you have said; I know you speak with authority and wisdom, but I know my people, and they know me. . . ."

He's blinded, Darenga thought. *He won't see.* "Where is Laatam now?" she asked him, wondering, finally, how it was they were not together.

"It was difficult, but I managed it," he answered.

It was all he intended to say, but she caught the suggestion of time limited and told him, "You said you sensed uneasiness, and I do, too."

She had to go carefully, had to convince herself as well. "The time isn't right for this . . . arrangement you suggest. Everything should be less fluid, not so high-pitched, when everyone is calm and things are back to normal. Do you see that the best thing for me to do is to go into the Yarbeen until this is over?"

He was silent a very long time, long enough for her to become acutely aware again of how close he stood to her, of the drift of honey fragrance in the still air of the room. "It will be fifty-six sunfalls before everything is finished and all Klada goes home."

"Not so very long, really. And you see, don't you? It's the most . . . prudent thing to do under the circumstances?"

"You would return immediately?"

"Yes, of course. Certainly."

Another deep and thoughtful pause that left her lungs aching for air. "On that promise, I will agree."

She made a slight turn, found herself free. And then she swung back to face him.

"Chaeya . . ." he said, as if he were grateful for that gesture.

"I don't really want to go, you know."

"Yes."

Oddly, it was the coolness of his skin that she noticed, the coolness of his skin and the light fragile structure of his body, like some fantastic bird that stood with folded wings as she caressed it, as she pressed with foolish instinct against the empty loins.

"Ah, M'landan," she said, turning her head away. "This is agony."

An aggrieved sound rose from his throat. "Let me do this for you . . . and for me."

And she thrust out her hands as if it were a reflex,

reaching for the pain before she could think of what it meant.

His fingers came swiftly down around her wrists, locking her palms against his even as the screens were flung aside and the deep tone he had begun died in his throat. The laanva poured into her hands and raced burning up her arms, exploding against her heart with Laatam's scream of outrage and Trolon's manic cry, *"Everything is defiled!"*

Like a curtain, the thick odor of honey surrounded them. Darenga sank her head against M'landan's shoulder, her eyes opening to the line of his throat and the fold of his hood where it shadowed both their faces.

"Chaeya," he murmured. "Remember . . . Chaeya—" and he was suddenly jerked away, leaving her teetering, off-balance, still trying to draw air into her lungs.

She stared around her, at the robed figures filling the room like death multiplied, at Trolon whirling a hinged harvest knife. M'Landan was being dragged toward the wall. His legs struck the ledge, and he half-fell into a sitting position and was immediately obscured in a swirl of robes.

Darenga swung to the side, crabbing forward, off-center. Her eyes were on Trolon, who, with Laatam burning at his side, shouted abuses. She grabbed the folds of material that encircled M'landan, and flung the nearest M'dians back. As the rest of the group then shifted, M'landan glimpsed her, cried out, "Chaeya! Don't hurt them! Don't hurt them!"

"Chaeya! He called her *Chaeya!"* Laatam screamed in a voice that pierced the air. *"Trolon!"* And it was both a command and a cry of vengeance.

"Stay away from him!" Darenga shouted as Trolon moved forward. "Stay away from him, Trolon!" Standard Maintainer, the language of command, old habits in a moment of extreme stress. Trolon didn't understand the words, but he recognized something in the tone, and he stopped, looked toward her, knife handle in one hand, the tip in the other.

"That's right, look at me," she said. "Look at me, Trolon—"

"Stop!" M'landan had regained his feet, still held by his captors, who tried to pull him down again, but he shook

54

them off. "Look to your priest! He is the one who must answer to this!"

"There's no answer you can give us, M'landan," Trolon cried, swinging back in his direction. "We saw this desecration! You poured the seed of your generations into the hands of that flesh-eater and left us barren!"

"There is enough—"

"How many times have you done this, M'landan?" Samar pushed his way forward into the ring around M'landan. "How many times?" And he shoved at him, but M'landan kept his balance.

"There is enough! I tell you all, our generations rest within me, and they are safe—"

Laatam let out a cry with a fierce upturn of force and emotion in her voice that raced through the stifling room. "The flesh-eater has held his attention since the time he was a child. He has been with her more than he has been with us. That answers your question, Samar!"

Now Darenga was being pressed back from the group that held M'landan, away from Trolon, who gripped the knife in his hands. She clasped her fingers together and brought her arms down on the M'dians closest to her, hurling the light bodies to the floor.

"Don't hurt them, I told you! Don't you understand me? Don't hurt them!"

She stopped, stood panting as a circle widened around her. But she had brought herself closer to Trolon, who now looked away from her to Laatam.

"She's trying to distract us," Laatam called out. "Turn away from her."

"Yes, Laatam, to me," M'landan replied. "I committed the offense against you."

"Against me? Against our generations! You've laid our fields to waste. You've ruined our city. You've left us beggars to plead at the robes of another priest. If we have children at all, it will be through the mercy of another city, and the children will bear this stigma."

"You will put a stigma on them, Laatam, if you persist in this. Do you think I would destroy my own species? Have you known me at all and think that?" The spell-voice in baritone anchoring Laatam at the edge of the crowd. He lowered his voice, lengthened the melody. "I have humiliated you, my sister; *mlo saindla*—" he began, his eyes intent on her. But Trolon pushed toward him, reached swiftly across the robed shoulders separating them, and struck him on the side of the head with the long thick handle of the knife.

"*My sister!*" Trolon raged. "You have no sisters!" He swung the handle down again. M'landan staggered, slumped his head for an instant, and then raised it again.

Darenga leaped forward. "*Trolon!*" she yelled and was slammed in the back by a blow that dropped her to her hands and knees. She shook her head, felt the quick rasp of a robe across her face.

Get to your feet! They'll kill you down here! Again she was struck on the back, and knew it was only the extra protection of her cloak that had saved her spine. She twisted, reached up and caught the handle as the M'dian standing over her swung the knife down. She wrenched it from his hands, came up on her knees with a harsh cry, and made a swift gashing circle with the broad metal blade. There was a howl of pain and a rush of figures away from her.

"Areia!" M'landan's voice, fear in it now.

She pulled herself to her feet, stood swaying with the knife drawn back, her eyes on the M'dians surrounding her, who poured out wild frequencies that tore at her ears and burned her eyes.

She heard M'landan cry, "The Yarbeen!" and turned to see Trolon against him, the crowd pushing them both back against the wall, and then the one word yelled out in a voice hardly his own, a word spoken in her language, harsh and commanding, that revealed nothing of the fear he felt for her safety, "*Go!*"

She hesitated, churning against the genetic demand for obedience. But the command came once more: "Go!" and the figures around her sank away as she dropped the knife and moved to the doorway, her eyes on the banded hood.

His voice flowed toward her once more, resigned and calm through the tumult around him. "Have your vengeance on me, my brother; but you will be the one to suffer."

She went through the screens, tearing them from their tracks and hurling them at the figures moving against the wall. Outside the room, there was a sudden hush as she appeared in the doorway, and the people crowding up the corridor flew aside to let her pass when they saw her face.

There was a sudden cessation of sound in the room behind her, but she didn't look back, and everything ahead was blurred. She stumbled, found herself at the entrance to the haruund and Tlaima in front of her.

"They're going to kill him," Darenga said. "Help him."

And Tlaima, in accusation and grief, "What have you done to us!"

There was no reply to that—under the two suns that shone quietly down, there was no reply she could give, and as Tlaima ran on past her into the building, Darenga turned blindly away toward the plain.

Chapter 5

At the slope of city and line of plain, Darenga stopped and looked back. A dreadful silence lay over everything; Death walking the eternal afternoon. She ranged back and forth on the sand, watching the haruund, her eyes roving over the walls, the window openings. There was nothing. No sound, no movement. Her pacing stopped. Slowly she backed away, entered the islands, faltered to a stop again, then finally swung around toward the distant shadow line.

She walked the soft yielding sand past the islands where the long waving grass sighed in the pulse of the wind. The M'dians stood in the deep purple grass, only the sheen of their eyes visible within their hoods, silent, the edges of their robes riffling softly. All across that great expanse they floated and droned monotonously, one tremendous chorus that held an everlasting note irreconcilable that lay stratified on the air like acrid smoke.

She reached the Yarbeen, plunged into its shadow. Behind her massed the islands, rocking on the green sea, softly drumming as the breeze funneled in and out of the empty bud sockets of L'M'dia.

She made her way back to her camp and beyond the cirque where she began to climb into a tall cluster of boulders that thrust some twenty-five yards into the dim air. The uppermost heel of rock was inaccessible, projecting above the rest of the formation, but Darenga was able to maintain a tenuous hold at its base, her bare feet wedged into the narrow ledge, her arms around a rough outcropping as if she were embracing it.

In the far distance, Ilanu glittered and swam in gold and silver starts. Nothing distinguishable but color and light. She lay her head against the rock, watching that shimmer in the rusty air.

I've done what you've commanded, a treachery you

didn't realize; that treachery of the blood that was meant to preserve.

She drew her head away from the rock, carefully, so she wouldn't disturb her balance, adjusted her eyes to the distant city, the pupils within the clear green irises fluctuating, sharpening the focus. Small grains of the loosened rock clung to the fine hairs of her cheek, flecks of brown against the faint scattering of freckles over her fair skin. Her hair, unbound, curved around her face and fell over her shoulders in a wild copper tangle that caught at the rough stone.

"What do I do now, M'landan? Dear God! What do I do now?"

And as she said it, the planet lurched, spun forward. She clung screaming to the pinnacle as it thrust out, soaring toward the inward edge of the shadow line, toward the stars that lay still and unperturbed in the great black firmament beyond the wide faint ring. The islands dropped away, reeling off to one side, tilting toward the curve of the planet's horizon. The city swerved; a pale gold tide winked around it. She clawed at the rock as it reached its apogee then tipped and shook her loose, shrieking as she plummeted down through the deep maroon twilight.

She opened her eyes to the toppling rock, jerked frantically to one side to escape. But it remained where it was, pressing up into the shadow, stationary, secure. She sat up with her head in her hands trying to remember . . . a movement of people like a pale and distant tide. She scrambled up, sprang to the foothold of the rock to stare toward Ilanu and the far slope. There it was, washed down from the slope and twinkling into the islands. She stared at it—the movement across that distance, barely perceptible.

They're coming after me! She dropped to the ground, landed in a crouch that she rose from tense and indecisive. After a moment, she settled slowly back into the rocks to wait.

It was more a sense of time passing that drew her back to alertness than any sound, for they arrived noiselessly, sifting through the islands like Baandla's nervous light. She stood up and came forward out of the outcropping to the edge of the shadow where the line was indefinite, wavering; a frail curtain shifting in the wind.

Like players entering from the wings, a few M'dians came in from either side. She noted their stance, the possibilities suggested in the way they approached her. There was no immediate threat there. They seemed merely to have arrived ahead of the rest. She waited with them in silence, her hands at her sides.

There are two of you that are going down with me, she thought, as she concentrated on the mass of islands just ahead. She breathed with slow deliberation, balancing the oxygen necessary for the few brief moments she would need. She would take Trolon first. . . .

But it was Laatam who appeared, moving forward unhesitatingly in a measured flow of robes and stopping some eight yards away, still in sunlight.

"Flesh-eater!" she addressed Darenga, and the tones and inflections she gave it meant *eater-of-children.*

No, Darenga thought, *you will be first.*

"What have you come for, Laatam? Your evil has already been done."

"There is evil and there is justice," she replied. "Justice seeks the light. The evil I see stands in the shadow where its deeds were conceived and worked."

There were more people arriving, coming up behind Laatam in the rufous air. Darenga perceived them assembling, but kept her eyes on Laatam.

"The only evil coming down this day was demanded by your ambition, Laatam." Ever so slightly, Darenga shifted her balance.

"*You!*" came a bellow from Trolon, then. Laatam turned quietly aside, and Darenga looked past her to where he and Samar stood with M'landan between them, hanging supported by their rough grip, his head sagging forward. A little way off, Tlaima and Klayon hovered distraught, their eyes on M'landan.

"You!" Trolon said again. "Here is our priest. Take what you can from him now!" And they dragged him stumbling forward.

Darenga stood mute, seeing that he lived, but knowing from his posture and the heavy, half-unconscious response of his body that he was grievously injured. The front folds of his robe were stained a pale green, like liquid jade, his sleeves saturated with it.

Suddenly, Trolon and Samar thrust him forward across the last few yards. He staggered, twisted, and fell against her as she caught his weight. He sank down to his knees, his head falling on his chest. Across her palms, his voice was a faint vibration. "Take me away from them . . . please."

"Now you have what you desire most, M'landan," Trolon said contemptuously.

Darenga raised her head and, with M'landan's weight still bending her forward, looked up at him. "What have you done to him?" she asked in a roil of notes that lay bare in her voice the assassin that peered out at him from her eyes.

Tlaima and Klayon had dropped down on either side of M'landan and put their arms around him, protective and fearful. Now Tlaima lay her long fingers on M'landan's sleeve and drew it back.

"His hands—" she cried out "—they've cut off his hands!"

Darenga started back, staring down at the foreshortened arm, the bindings wet, pale liquid green, with his blood. She pushed back the other sleeve, saw the drenched cloth and gave a sudden unintelligible cry as she let his weight be supported by Klayon and Tlaima and came erect.

"Do nothing more," M'landan said, unable to lift his head. And then, "Please . . . stop her."

Trolon had swept back to Laatam and Samar, and now the group retreated, the rest of the M'dians moving with them, drifting back into the islands.

"You'd murder him with contempt, Trolon?" She advanced onto the plain, breaking out of the shadow line in a sudden radiance of bronze and copper, her wild hair shot and blazing in Yamth's light as she bore down on him.

"You're going to die, Trolon."

Tlaima flew up beside her. "You can't do this!"

"We know who the killers of our children are," cried Laatam, fierce in her righteousness. "We know who causes our desolation. This is proper justice. If he lives he will spend every sunfall with the destruction he has caused his people laid before his eyes. And he will hate you with every breath he takes. There—in that fitting darkness where you both belong." With a gesture that would have drawn Trolon along with her, she turned. But Darenga had moved swiftly and cut him away from the group.

"Now, Trolon," she said quietly.

Tlaima flung herself against the bronze cloak, knotted

her fingers into the material. "Don't do this! You must not do this!"

"Let go!"

"There has been enough for us to suffer; don't add to this terrible misery!"

"I said, let go of me!"

"M'landan's life is draining into the sand, and you would have your revenge as he dies! Oh, you are cruel to do this to him!"

Darenga looked away then from Trolon to Tlaima, who had released her and stood with her hands at her sides, poised in anxiety.

"Please," Tlaima said. "You think only of yourself."

Trolon swung quickly away to join Laatam. Darenga raised her head, but made no move to pursue him. "This doesn't end it, Trolon," she called as the pair retreated into the islands with the remainder of the M'dians. "Do you hear me, Laatam? *This doesn't end it!*"

She turned to Tlaima, said savagely, "They'll sleep with that knife between them until I bury it in both of them." She saw the horror in Tlaima's face. It was too familiar, that recognition of murder. She swung away and strode quickly to where Klayon was trying to bring M'landan to his feet.

"Let me have him," she told Klayon. She cradled M'landan in her arms, lifted up the light body, and heard him moan softly in pain. His head rolled against her shoulder. His hood had been torn off, ripped away with the purple bands; all across that long expanse of plain, there had been no protection for his head.

She brought him down the slope into the cirque and lay him on the sand while she removed her cloak and spread it out. Then she lifted him onto it and sat down beside him.

At the edges of the cloak, Klayon and Tlaima stood silently, tears long since spent, stood with their fingers locked in front of them, and Darenga wondered if it were for fear of the Yarbeen that they assumed that pose, or the sense of death approaching.

"Forgive my people," M'landan said, looking up at her. "Forgive me."

"Don't talk, M'landan. Rest, please."

There was more he wanted to say, but he accepted her soft command and was silent.

It became a vigil of pain as well as death, for although he didn't speak, he made the periodic and restless movements all creatures with extreme injuries make. From deep inside his throat a low vibration came now and then, and she knew his cries were audible to Klayon and Tlaima by the disquieted way they moved to attend him, and then drew back because there was nothing that could be done.

She changed the bandages on his arms with wadding and strips torn from the inner lining of her robe, deploring the pain he suffered when she did it, but knowing the slow seeping away of his blood couldn't keep on much longer if he were to have a chance at all.

It took a deep and heavy toll on her rigid self-discipline to unwind the cloth and finally bring her eyes on that mutilation. All the while he lay with his face averted, the great dull eyes staring at the cirque wall.

Once she had applied the pressure pad and finished the neat and careful bandages, he seemed to rest more comfortably, although a glistening film that could not be wiped away remained on his skin, a reminder of the dangerous loss of fluids from his body. So Darenga insisted that he drink water, although the moisture he could absorb was appallingly little compared to what he had lost.

It was several hours before she would leave his side, and then only because the water container was empty. As soon as she rose, Tlaima and Klayon sank down beside him, having stood all the long hours at the edge of her cloak in what she suddenly realized was an act of deference to her. And it lowered spirits already ebbed to despair that she had left them standing.

She followed the sloping terrain into a small arroyo where a spring welled up clear among a small group of rocks. Water-loving flora crowded at the edges, delicate little cushions that grew up into the surrounding rocks as far as the evaporating water drifted. Lovely, dependent little plants that existed nowhere else. She dipped the container into the pool, letting it fill as the ripples lapped over the moss.

She was tired, exhausted; everything wrung out. Bone dry. She set the container in the sand and folded down on her haunches, the robe billowing out around her, and lay her head against her knees. From a center of absolute zero inside her, the cold spread out until she was shaking so badly she had to brace her hand on the ground to keep her balance. Above her, and beyond the deeps of the shadow line, the stars faintly glittered in the greater immensity that was such a mystery to him and so well understood by her; and to what she knew of it and its vast uncertainties she appealed in weary desperation, *Let him live, let him live.*

When she returned, Tlaima and Klayon rose, and would have gone to their position at the edge of the cloak, but she told them, "Please . . . don't stand up anymore." And, hearing the edge to her voice, they silently seated themselves on either side of M'landan. Then, for the first time, M'landan closed his eyes and was still.

Darenga surged forward, scanning his face, and would have touched him, but Tlaima held up her hand.

"He's sleeping," she said softly.

Darenga sank back against her heels, staring at him, still a little alarmed by his motionless form, until she finally detected the slow rise and fall of his chest. "Are you sure?"

"Yes," Klayon answered. "It is the best thing for him, if his body is to heal."

There was a long silence. Then Darenga said, "If his body is to heal, he'll have to have food," thinking that everything was reversed, her food source here, his back there, and no return for him to Ilanu. "What can we do about it? Where can we get the food he needs—that you need?"

"We have portions that are ours," Tlaima said.

"But weren't you turned out of the city, too?"

"We did nothing," Klayon said. "They can't cast us out. This is our duty—to stay with our priest. But he is also our brother, and what they did to him was wrong. Even if it were not our duty, we would have come with him." Bitterness and helplessness: *I would have helped him if I could.* He looked across at her silently, and she answered that silence.

"I know my part in this; I have no excuses to give you for it, except M'landan and I understood each other too late."

"I blamed you unfairly," Tlaima said. "You cannot help that you exist. Perhaps the understanding you speak of only intensified what had drawn you together."

It was true, of course, for even had she been able to leave unnoticed from his chamber, and even though he had, in those last few moments, consented to what he knew was her effort to free herself and him, she would have come back. And he would have welcomed her. The inevitable would only have been delayed. *Destruction wherever I go.*

"We can go back to the city," Klayon said, following the direction of her first question. "They can't refuse us our portion. They must give us our share of food and other things we need."

"And of course they wouldn't give anything to M'landan?"

"No. But what Tlaima and I have together will be enough."

"Isn't there a danger to you?"

"No. We have carried out our duty; there's no offense in that."

They had been speaking in low tones, but M'landan stirred and they fell silent. Presently, Tlaima rose, gesturing for Klayon to follow, and they walked a way off and stood talking. Darenga turned back to M'landan, watching the slow breathing, the bruised and glistening skin.

When Tlaima touched her shoulder and motioned for her, Darenga started to her feet, but M'landan's eyes came open and a low indefinite melody rose from his throat.

"We'll be back by fourth sunfall," Tlaima whispered, and, with a gentle pressure on Darenga's shoulder, set her back down again.

She would have protested their journey back to Ilanu—they were both exhausted and, no matter what they said, she felt there was a danger—but M'landan would need food if he were to survive, and it might be easier to get it now than later.

He was trying to speak to her. "You must not think to avenge me; you must promise me this." It had filled his mind; the fear that she would cause harm, she realized that, but it was too soon, too fresh for her to be able to make such a promise.

"Please rest, M'landan."

He closed his eyes briefly, made a sideways movement with his head. "You evade, you evade," he said, distraught. He tried to rise, but fell back with a cry when his bandaged arms touched the ground.

"I can't promise you something your language will reveal a lie!" she cried. "All I can tell you is that I won't do anything now!"

No solace in that. He lay very still with his eyes focused at a point above her head where there was nothing but the rim of the cirque and the glimmering shadow. Finally he said, "Perhaps in my joy at recognizing what we have in common I was blinded to our differences. I cannot ask of you what is impossible for you to give."

There were nuances faintly audible; she was a being from a hard and brilliant culture, who knew violent things, who could predict the violence he had been so ravaged by and ill-prepared for; she had known it would happen.

He continued to stare up at the dark above the cirque, his eyes lusterless. The slight movements that were the indicators of his pain began again, and Darenga, sitting quietly beside him, was unable to help him or herself.

When Tlaima and Klayon returned, twelve hours later, they were pulling a hand cart filled with provisions. Darenga had heard it coming—the slow creak of its wheels —long before M'landan did.

In all of Ilanu, no one oiled a cart wheel to prevent the noise, although the oil extracted from L'M'dia was one of the finest oils in all the known worlds. The sound was pleasant to them, like the sounds of birds on Earth or Ronadjoun, or the song of the winnowale in the water races of Vrega. She had no such association. The screak of a wheel was the screak of a wheel, something to measure distance between it and the sleeping figure she guarded.

M'landan had finally fallen into a deep and motionless slumber, and Darenga, exhausted and fearing hallucination, had fallen asleep at a distance from him, her back against the cirque wall, her head dropped forward, her wrists dangling over her knees.

She had struggled up out of a nightmare of sound and devastation to a sudden half-crouching alertness as she strained to identify the noise that had wakened her. Then in a few seconds she had recognized it and come to her feet, still listening, judging the distance. A mile, possibly more. She went to M'landan, saw that he still slept, and walked swiftly up the incline to stand at the keyhole entrance to the chamber looking out toward the plain.

"Areia?"

66

She turned and came back down the slope. "It's Tlaima and Klayon," she told him, kneeling down. "They've brought supplies. We'll be able to make you more comfortable now."

He stirred a little at that, his eyes clearing slightly. "They went to Ilanu? They should have waited."

"I'm going to help them unload, M'landan. I'll only be a few minutes. Would you like some water before I go?"

"Please . . . a little."

He raised his head as she slipped her arm behind him, supporting him as she brought the bowl to his swollen mouth. The dark bruises along the side of his head above the ear membrane marked where Trolon had struck him with the knife handle. But there were other bruises on his face; she knew with a cold knowledge borne of experience that they had been acting out their anger on him as they had pulled him through the islands.

Strangely, instead of rage there was a swift downturning inside her; she felt the rancor stripping away and some overwhelming sense she couldn't identify taking its place. She began to cry, without any idea why she would do this, but it would not be suppressed. She put her cheek against his forehead, trying not to hold him too tightly, but desperately needing that closeness.

"I'm sorry . . . I'm sorry," she said. "It was your command. I was helpless—I couldn't do anything," as he was saying, "*Mlo saindla, mlo saindla*," and trying to raise his arms and crying too.

It was several minutes later that he said quietly, "We must try to understand this. The gods do not act without mercy. There is a wider purpose to this tragedy that has been worked on us." The tone and deep rhythm in his voice comforted, was healing, was meant to heal himself as well as her. So she sat with his head cradled in her arms, listening to the sound and understanding the words to be the strength he gave himself.

After a time she lowered his head and stood up. "I'd better help them unload," she told him. The noise of the wheels had stopped some moments before and she could hear Tlaima and Klayon now. "I'll be back in a few minutes."

"Yes, go ahead. I'll be all right."

Tlaima and Klayon had brought the cart near her campfire area. As she came up, Klayon was gingerly removing a large ornate jar from a carefully padded section of the cart. He saw her coming and knelt down to uncap the jar and, with extreme care, pour some of it into a small vial that he held out to her. The liquid inside was amber-colored.

"What is it?" she asked, turning it in her fingers. Something of great value, by his careful actions.

"Lumeena, the liquid of the globe," he answered.

The substance that filled the hollow globe of L'M'dia and from which the major portion of nourishment for the M'dians was taken and processed. "It is very concentrated. Taken in small quantities it is very beneficial." He set the jar out of the way, mounded the sides with sand to keep it steady.

"Do I give it to him this way, or should I add water to it?"

Klayon the physician; the M'dians would feel the loss of him.

"No, not water. Here, take this to him." He handed her a small hanj pod, about one quart. Something for the pain. "He must drink it all first, and then the lumeena."

She turned quickly and went back to the cirque while Klayon and Tlaima began unloading the rest of the cart.

When M'landan saw what she carried in her hands there was obvious relief in his face.

"All of it," she told him, as she filled a bowl with the fermented liquor, then lifted his head a little so his tongue could reach the liquid. "Klayon's orders."

He was a while draining the bowl, but once he had, he relaxed his arms from their rigid position across his chest and lay them alongside his body. His eyes were suddenly brilliant, a convex mirror upon which all images struck bright and clear.

She felt a sudden buoyancy. "There's more," she told him. "You haven't finished yet."

The swollen mouth broadened slightly. "No more hanj," he protested weakly.

"Not hanj," she said, bringing up the amber-filled vial, "lumeena. The prescription says it's to follow the first medicine." She knew he had no idea what she was talking about, but just saying something flippant after the unrelieved despair of the past hours was reason enough for saying it. He drank obediently, sucking up the last of it as

Klayon and Tlaima came down into the cirque with rolls of cloth they dropped near the wall. As Tlaima began smoothing the fabric out into beds, Klayon came over to them and stood for a moment, looking down at M'landan, with his hands tucked solemnly inside his sleeves. M'landan stared back up at him.

"The hanj is working, eh, M'landan?"

"Too much, my brother," he answered, the notes slurring.

"Just the right amount," Klayon replied. "I'm never wrong."

There was an exaggeratedly long tone from M'landan that was the equivalent of *hmmmm* in human speech. "You make me float too far on this tide."

"It's what you need, my brother."

"Yes, perhaps you're right." M'landan turned his head toward Darenga, then back to Klayon. "Please, I want you all to sleep. The pain is reduced now, and I am resting comfortably. There is nothing more for us to do but rely on the gods and the healing power they have placed in my body. Please, all of you rest."

They reluctantly conceded that what he said was true, and Klayon and Tlaima lay down on their rolls of fiber and cloth, and Darenga finally put her head down beside M'landan's where she could open her eyes and instantly see the series of curves that was his profile.

Once he turned his head to look at her with his great flashing eyes, then returned to his study of the stars above the cirque rim. Very low, barely audible to her, came a soft repetitive melodic line. She fell asleep listening to it.

Chapter 6

At the end of seventy-two hours, M'landan was able to sit comfortably in a sort of chair they had fashioned for him from the hand cart and the abundance of cloth brought back from Ilanu. He had done some walking, which Klayon felt necessary to his bodily functions, but their main concern was to build back his strength.

The regimen was nourishment and water. Hanj was no longer necessary because there was only minor pain now and M'landan preferred it to the reeling disorientation of the liquor, under the influence of which he had sung a great deal, but which still made him uncomfortable.

There had been the question of hood replacement for his robe. Tlaima had brought them each an extra garment and the discussion had arisen during an examination of them. Darenga, deeply angered by the removal of the bands from M'landan's hood, and his refusal to have them replaced even though Tlaima had managed to get some of the sacred material, was determined that his status as priest be preserved. "If you won't wear purple," she told him, "then you'll wear the colors of Yamth and Baandla, because you were chosen by your gods, not your people."

He had looked at her, astounded. The anger was there in the undertones of her voice, but it was restrained and purposeful, her mention of the gods respectful. He watched with the others as she spread her wide cloak on the sand and removed a long section from it that she handed to Klayon.

"Use this for his hoods," she told him.

When Klayon had fashioned one of the hoods and attached it to the robe M'landan wore, Darenga lifted it over his head. "Wear this hood with dignity, M'landan," she said, while the three stood transfixed by this clear and ringing declaration. "Your gods approve."

At the next first sunfall, Darenga went to the spring to refill the water container. She returned quietly up the slope and was already into the keyhole to the cirque before she saw the figures grouped together like an ancient religious painting—Tlaima and Klayon kneeling before the chair where M'landan sat with his face turned upward as he chanted in a low voice.

Darenga swung quickly away from the entrance and made her way along the outer rocks of the chamber, where she stopped, set the container down and crouched beside it, resting her forehead against her knee.

They had waited until she had left before M'landan performed this rite, whatever it was. She felt as if she had stepped into the bedroom of friends who were in the heat of intercourse.

She raised her head and sat looking out into the maroon shadows wondering exactly what she had expected. After all, he was a priest. Hadn't she spoken the little piece that acknowledged what he was? Provided the hood that distinguished him? She might be useless, having shed her responsibilities and duties together with the honors that had been the mantle of her authority, but even though his parish members had shrunk to two, there was still need for him. He would still carry out what obligations he could and praise his gods for allowing him that. Too bad, too bad she had gone so naked away from her own life. Like the ancient Egyptians of Earth, she could have used a few trinkets for the journey.

M'landan was much better now. He could get around the camp without becoming faint, and his appetite was improving. Klayon, in his role as physician, ministered to many of his needs, but Darenga poured water and food for him, although he could manage now to lift the bowl himself. It had taken a few disastrous trials for him to accomplish this, but he had gone about it with a good humor that took much of the tension out of watching him struggle to perform even this simple act by himself.

To Tlaima fell the responsibility for his robes, a task that had always been hers, and she and Klayon jointly oversaw the cleanliness of his body, a rite which was equally a religious and personal aesthetic. There was the ritual bath every first sunfall, the robes discarded, the pale and slender body lathered and turning like a perfect mandrake root. He was not self-conscious, and neither were Tlaima and Klayon, and the three exchanged some brilliant and witty conversation during this ceremony. M'landan's great dark eyes would fall occasionally on Darenga, but she always dropped her gaze. And suffered every time she did. No amount of self-chastising seemed to help. Finally she simply feigned sleep, which ravished her pride, but the sight of him unclothed disturbed her too much, and what was there for her to say that would not bring to ruin what pride she had left? But then, everything about him disturbed her far more than she was willing to fully admit.

One fourth sunfall, she was up, alternately pacing the campground and sitting and staring at the ashes of a fire that had gone out long before, when, suddenly at the edge of the site, there appeared a M'dian. She had been sitting; now she rose slowly, alert instantly, evaluating his posture, testing the air.

He stood quietly, hands in sleeves, watching her as she watched him. She recognized him as one of the weavers. Finally he asked in a voice timid with hope, "Does he live?"

She straightened, her hands going to rest on her hips. "Are there any more of you?"

"No. No, I'm the only one."

"What do you want with him?" Both answer and warning.

He looked as if he were going to cry. He stepped quickly toward her, drawing out his hands from his sleeves in an unexpected movement that almost cost him a severe blow.

"Please," he said, "may I see him?"

"He's asleep," she answered hoarsely, because he had startled her.

Now he stood with his hands extended slightly outward from his body, a M'dian gesture of agitation. "May I wait, then? May I wait here?"

There was a desperation in his voice that made her hesitate refusing him. She thought, *M'landan would want to see him.*

She said, "Follow me," and, turning abruptly, led him around toward the entrance of the cirque. At the upslope

72

she told him, "Wait here," and came up into the entrance-way and stopped.

M'landan had heard, of course, and had gotten up from the cloak and was now seated in the chair. And she wondered if it were his intuitive sense of the dramatic that had placed him there, or a need to retain the dignity that had been so cruelly taken from him. Perhaps both. Whatever the reason, the result was the same, and she saw it through her eyes and the eyes of the M'dian who came up as she gestured to him, who stood staring down into the cirque where, in the richly-woven drapery of the chair, M'landan sat composed and shadowy, the bronze threads in his hood gleaming and shifting with the movement of his slow breathing.

"Why have you come, Treaden?" he asked, and even though he spoke quietly, there was a faint echo from the walls.

Darenga watched as Treaden moved down into the cirque in a stiff, disjointed walk, as if he were afraid to approach the figure sitting there and yet was compelled to do so. When he was still a yard's length from the chair, he flung himself to the ground and gripped M'landan's knees with his hands.

"My priest—*mlo saindla*, please, *mlo saindla*. I am so sorry for what I have done to you!"

As the weaver cried this out, Tlaima and Klayon, who had come instantly to their feet when they had heard Darenga speaking at the doorway, now moved to positions at either side of the chair and stood unmoving as they waited for M'landan's reply.

He drew his arms from his sleeves and rested them in his lap. The bronze gauntlets he now wore over the stumps of his wrists reflected the same soft fire as his hood. The M'dian pulled his head back, but still clutched M'landan's knees, his fingers frozen inches from the bronze stumps.

"But you were justified," M'landan answered in his deep and formal baritone.

"No, my priest, there was no justice in that. You were not given a chance to speak."

"I violated our laws. Everyone who entered my chamber at that moment saw the violation."

"Yes, I saw the violation myself."

"And you helped carry out the sentence on me, Treaden,"

he said quietly. "You must have thought the punishment correct; you held my arms down, even though I told you I would hold them still for Trolon's knife—" He looked up as Darenga started down the slope, and said in a tone that arrested her in mid-stride, "Do not enter. Return to the doorway."

When she had slowly backed away, her eyes on Treaden, who had pressed closer to M'landan as she had come toward him, he turned his head down to the weaver again.

"Was the punishment not correct?"

"It seemed so at the time. Everything was confused and ugly, and the air was thick with fragrance. . . ."

A convoluted translation from the ITU: her own understanding of the M'dian language made his phrase to be, "the odor of the priest's communion; conception."

Darenga pulled back further into the shadow of the doorway, burning with shame. *God! What's wrong with me? I should strangle him where he kneels.*

"If you thought the punishment just," M'landan was saying, "why do you come to me now?"

"Oh, my priest, I know it was wrong. It has never left my mind that you tried to speak and were struck into silence. You have never done your people any offense. This would have been explained, I know. You would not destroy us."

Treaden lifted the bronze gauntlets, held them against his ear membranes. "*Mlo saindla!*" he cried again. "*Mlo saindla!* There is no rest for me. Please, my priest!"

"There will be no comfort from these," M'landan answered gently, and drew his arms back. "If you find no fault in me, what of her?" And he lifted one gauntlet toward the entrance where Darenga stood in the shadows.

Treaden turned his head, and she saw his eyes go dull. "I tried to blame her, my priest," he said. "But you called her Chaeya, and I heard the love and fear in your voice, and I saw her struggle to reach you. . . ."

His voice dropped. "And I saw her obey against her will when you told her to leave." He turned his gaze back to M'landan. "I see her now ready to protect you even as Tlaima and Klayon at your side. You would have made clear to us your reasons if you had been allowed to speak. And now it is too late. We will be the last generation." He began to weep then, his forehead pressed against his hands.

No one moved until M'landan, with the flat end of his gauntlets, raised Treaden's head. "My brother," he said, in the quietly echoing chamber, "you were forgiven when those words left your mouth." He turned his face upward and, in the ringing tone of invocation, called, "*Sai Baandla, Sai Yamth* whose light penetrates even into this darkness, see this one and give him the warmth of your forgiveness, knowing that I who suffered his violence have forgiven him. Grant him peace."

Softly, in counterpoint, Tlaima and Klayon: "Grant him peace, O Gods."

Treaden rose, too overcome to do more than press his hands against M'landan's knees and look long and searchingly at Tlaima and Klayon. He backed away, turned, and started up the slope. Darenga stood against the rock of the entrance, watching him, and he slowed as he saw her, but then went past as she turned aside, her green eyes burning coldly after him.

M'landan came up beside her. "I was harsh, forgive me. But it was important that he not be frightened away."

"Or killed?" she replied in a labored tone.

"I did not believe you would harm him, even though your anger was apparent. But you might have frightened him away, and he would have suffered greatly for not receiving absolution."

"I can't feel sympathy for his problem. Contrition is an excuse, not a state of blessedness evoked by gods."

He pressed his wrist against her shoulder as she started to turn away. "You reason with a dichotomy of mind, Areia; you pronounce me chosen, and then deny what has made the choice."

"I'm not going to argue religion with you, M'landan. I said your gods chose you because that's how you perceive it." She looked away, angry without knowing why.

He accepted what she said silently, then told her, "Treaden is not a bad person, and he is appalled at what he did. Do you think his regret is ungenuine?"

"I'm hardly the one to measure his regret—I'm too aware of his crime."

"And our crime?" he asked softly. "Are we the only ones to be forgiven our passion?"

"Stop it, M'landan," she said, and walked away.

* * *

75

She awoke slowly, drowsily aware of M'landan leaning over her, shadowy and indistinct. "Are you going to sleep now?" she murmured.

"Yes," he answered quietly, but didn't move.

Inside his hood, darkness. "What is it?" she asked. But there was no answer from that folded backness. She reached out her hands into the emptiness of the hood, felt the warm curves of his face. "Is there something wrong?"

"No, nothing is wrong."

She started to lift herself, but he raised his arm slightly, and she relaxed back against the cloak. "Why are you looking at me?"

There was an untranslatable tone from him, and, after a moment, he lay down, adjusted his robes, crossed his arms into his sleeves, and stared up at the sky, what light there was captured in a shining crescent over his eye. "Sometimes I don't know what to say to you."

"Say what's on your mind," she said sharply, remembering the earlier scene in the entranceway. "I won't do anything to your people," she told him. "But only because it would be painful to you." In a hard run of notes she added "Whatever pain I could give them would be too momentary, anyway."

The light flashed and curved along his eyes as his head turned to her. "Why do you find it so difficult to forgive?"

The low question vibrated on the still air. Beyond M'landan near the wall, Darenga saw Klayon turn slowly in his sleep.

"It is very . . . . cleansing, to forgive," he said when she didn't answer.

She replied, "There are acts that one person commits against another that can be understood and forgotten—like harm done accidentally, or harm done with provocation, or injury caused in a dispute that gets out of control. But this was a contemptuous, murderous *insult*, and it can't be forgiven. Not by me. You should have sent Treaden away. Let *him* appeal to the gods for succor. He would have received the answer he deserved."

M'landan came up onto his elbow to stare down at her. "No one can appeal to Yamth and Baandla except through me. I thought you knew that. I am the stalk through which the words of Yamth and Baandla are spoken. His answer did come from the gods."

Now she came up. "And what do they say, M'landan? What does a ball of flaming helium and a mass of electrons have to say?"

He twisted his head slightly against the harsh quality of her song. "They tell me to be patient with you. And that has its own difficulties."

"Oh, it does," she said, and dropped back to the cloak and crossed her arms over her chest.

"You cause a turbulence in me sometimes that is unpleasant," he told her on one long level note. "I experience it with no one else." He touched her arms with one gauntlet. "We seem to share this feeling. Look, you draw your arms together to bar me out."

She relaxed then, let her arms slide down the curve of her body until her hands rested loosely one on the other. "I'm not trying to shut you out . . . exactly. It bothers me, if you want me to be honest—"

"Yes, of course, I want you to be honest."

"You're intelligent, with an open, discerning mind. But you keep clinging to these superstitions—you've seen Yamth and Baandla when you were on the Galaxy, seen them through the spectromes. Yamth is fire, damn it! You've seen that. Baandla is a mass of shrinking electrons. You understood all that, how the hell can you . . . prattle about forgiveness from them for people who cut off your goddamn hands!"

"They are manifestations of what is unseeable," he said, drawing back. He looked away from her. After a moment he said quietly, "There have been instances when I have stood next to you and spoke and you heard nothing." He was silent, then added, "As I was doing just now."

"Well—"

"Put your hand on my throat," he told her. "Yes, right there. Now. . . ."

There was a rapid thrumming against her palm and fingertips.

"You see?" The vibration slowed as he spoke aloud.

She lifted her hand away, placed it on her hip. "I felt the movement, yes."

"Yet you heard nothing?"

"No, but—"

"And yet Klayon can hear it. . . ." He turned his head toward the sleeping figures at the opposite wall.

Klayon rose up. "What?" he said, pushing back his hood from where it had twisted across his face. "What're you talking about, M'landan?"

"*Mlo saindla*, Klayon. A little conversation we're having. Go back to sleep."

"Well, I will," Klayon answered, and fell back into his bed.

"All right, I appreciate your demonstration. But your vocal chords can vibrate at frequencies my ears can't pick up. There's nothing mysterious about that."

"Of course not. I'm illustrating that just as you cannot hear what I sometimes say to you, neither can Klayon or Tlaima or Treaden hear what the gods speak to them. Only I can do that, and that is a great and beautiful mystery. So you see, if we can come back to our original point, I can forgive my people because, although I have suffered great physical pain, they will suffer more for having removed themselves from the gods."

After a moment, Darenga said, "Ah, M'landan, you take all the argument out of me." And she set aside her explanations of the voices he heard, the recorded data on occult and parapsychological phenomena; set it aside because she realized then that it was her own phantoms she had to deal with, that the abrasion came not from his religious beliefs but from her own slipping sense of identity, the fragments left of the person she had once been.

"I've been incredibly boorish, M'landan, trying to argue with you; it's a breach of every idea of good form in the Galaxy. And a Maintainer does not interfere with the culture of a planet, nor try to influence changes from established customs or religion." She smiled. "That's a quote. Even an ex-Maintainer can see the value in a rule like that."

"Yes, there is value in such a rule," he replied gravely. "I have only this more to say on the subject: the link with my gods is no longer perfect; I cannot, obviously, perform certain important rites or provide the laanva for the sacred liturgies. I can be useful in only minor ways now, except for two things only I can do for my people, and those are to forgive them when they are ready, and to be the channel through which my gods speak to them. These things I must do as long as I'm needed. There is no other way for me. No other way."

She leaned forward, reached into his hood to lay her

hands on his ear membranes. "Do you know how desperately sorry I am that this happened? How I would do anything to change it?"

His head bowed slightly within the light pressure of her fingers. "What would you change?"

"Everything, M'landan. I would go back to the beginning and change it all."

"How would you do it?" His voice was soft, lilting in a minor key, sadness underlying the melodic line. "Where would you begin, my arrogant Chaeya, to assume my guilt as well as your own?"

He raised his head as her hands came slowly away.

"I'm not trying to assume anyone's guilt. But if I hadn't come back none of this would have happened. You do see that, don't you?"

"I see the images you offer. The reality is that you did come back. And things happened just as they did. Each of us contributed; each of us is guilty to some degree. But none of us has ever had the power to change everything— or rather, all of us had equally the chance to change something of what happened. Do you see? Events happened as they did. They happened; we were affected, and we effected events. That only is the measure of our guilt, not what we might have done. Allow me my burden as I allow you yours; allow my people theirs."

"Allow me my identity. I am not M'dian, I'm human. I'm my own human past and this present." She lay back suddenly into the molded sand and brought her arm across her eyes. "There are responsibilities in both that I see with perfect clarity."

"You carry a heavy guilt from that past. It's time you laid it down."

"It's not guilt I feel, M'landan. What I did had to be done . . . they had caused so much destruction. . . . No guilt was involved."

He said nothing to that, but let her thoughts move her along in the silence. Then he said, "Do you think I want to change you?"

She answered, "You . . . press me. I feel you manipulating me."

He considered that, then denied it. "I told you once before I would not try to work against your will. I realize, perhaps more than you do, how vulnerable you are. . . ."

Vulnerable. Yes, vulnerable. Me—dependent on him.

He prodded her arm away from her face, and then rested the blunt gauntlet on the ground beside her head. His sleeve lay against her cheek. Along her side she could feel the slow rhythm of his heart. She looked up at him.

"We have not touched for a long time, Chaeya," he said in a long low melody that drew a brief corresponding tone from her throat. She reached up again into the hood, slid her hands into the darkness to feel the warm, rounded face, see the faint gloss that marked his eyes.

"I've wanted to. . . ." Too much revealed, too much compacted fear and despair suddenly released.

"Yes, I've seen it in your eyes. It vibrates through every song you make to me. You speak it in your sleep—"

"—in my sleep!"

"Yes." He leaned down and touched his mouth to hers, drew its long curve back and forth, the edges of his hood folding and unfolding rhythmically against the sides of her head, sequences of dim light and darkness and the faint scent of honey.

She lay very still in the rhythms of the hood and the swaying pressure on her chest and the movement he made to keep his balance.

"La'va Lai," he said. *Don't speak.*

The phrase was lyric and motion. *La'va Lai, La'va Lai.*

"Draw up your robes," he told her softly, stopping the rhythm, moving away.

She felt his hood fold against her thigh, and then his tongue probing, inserting, and then the gentle rhythm again. She clutched at his hood, said his name, twice, involuntarily, her body contracting over the withdrawing tongue, turning itself inside out after it. There was sudden relief that rocked her and made her faint, a wash of relief that drained her mind and body. She lay for a long time with her arms flung across her face, and then she got up and stumbled over to where M'landan sat with his back against the stone wall, his arms in his sleeves, his head bowed.

"Please," he said, as he felt her hand cup against the side of his head. "Please, a moment." Then across the small distance she made between them, " When you spoke . . . my own need . . . I must have a moment."

"I'm sorry, I thought—"

The hood turned toward her, the voice clear from the

shadow, "They cut off my hands; they did not cut away my passion or drain the seed from my body. I can serve your desire for me only if you are silent." He bowed his head again, muffling the minor phrase, "There is no release for me. Sometimes I think I will explode from it."

Darenga wrapped her arms around her knees and dropped her head forward with a moan.

He lay his gauntlet on her arm immediately. "*Mlo saindla;* I was indulging myself. The situation is not impossible I'm not unsatisfied in this, Chaeya. It is pleasant for me to touch you and taste the parts of your body; I know it gives you release, and it is all I can do for you. That is satisfaction for me. But when you speak, you use the melodies and tones of communion, and my body responds to these quite independent of my will."

"How do we handle this!" she said, and couldn't prevent the despair from sliding into her voice.

"It may not be what you would like, but it is what we have to share. It is enough for me—please let it be enough for you. It is not an empty gesture I make. The nature of our species restricts our contact, but be thankful we can meet at all across this difference."

The notes flowed out from the dim and running fire about his head that was as lightning seen from a distance. He put out his arm, and she moved into its curve and lay her head against his throat. "It seems at once strange and yet natural that we should develop this love and want to preserve it."

"And the damage we've caused in trying to preserve it—"

"That is the first time you've admitted *we*," he said, pressing his mouth against her hair. "Do you know that?"

"It's not an admission—"

"Concession, then. We share this burden; this chain of circumstance and action. So do my people. We were at the center, but they took on themselves the outcome. This is what they must all recognize for their own salvation."

"Is that what you were leading Treaden to—an admission of his guilt?"

"Not exactly; the recognition of the limits of everyone's responsibility in this, which includes his own. No one need accept any more than their own share, but they must also recognize exactly the measure of responsibility that rests with everyone else, and not attribute more or less than their true share. If they covet one grain of resentment against another because that would make their own guilt less, then they are cut off from the gods by their untruthfulness. If they assume one grain more of another's guilt, they suffer the gods' silence because of their arrogance. Absolution is a very exacting sacrament; it can be given only when the one who would receive it understands as if he or she sees in crystal the total measure of responsibility."

She realized then why it had seemed important to him that she—not be so arrogant? Wasn't that what he'd been saying? And she was oddly touched by his effort to reconcile her with his gods. For anyone who came within his sphere, he was tolerant and deeply concerned. *You would have made a bright and desperately needed addition to the Alliance*, she thought, and wondered why that had come to her mind.

She replied to him, "Is that ever possible?"

Her head was resting on the fold of his hood, and so she couldn't see his face, but she could hear his voice, feel the vibration of his song. "Yes, however, for some it is very difficult. But I will help any who will ask."

"And you think more will come?"

One of his arms lay along her hip where she sat half turned against his side. The other lay in his lap, the gauntlet running the same fire as his hood. It lifted slightly as he spoke. "I'm sure of it. Treaden was greatly disturbed, and there are others who will feel the same."

If that's true, it may be dangerous. We'll have to be careful. . . .

They talked for some time, until her eyelids became heavy and finally closed. She heard him say, "Everything is different now; there are no guidelines from tradition. All my instruction must come from the gods, and they are silent even with me, at times. But my people must accept what we have accepted. . . ."

She tried to keep her attention on what he was saying, and yet the warmth of his body, the strange and undefinable comfort in the curve of his arm, the relaxation he had given her, all conspired to make her sleepy so that she heard: "There must be a ceremony," and drowsily replied, "Yes, a ceremony. For what?" and didn't hear the answer to her question.

Chapter 7

She roused herself when she heard Tlaima speak softly to M'landan, recognizing immediately that it was well into first sunfall, but she didn't come fully awake until he had risen and had reached the cirque entrance.

"M'landan? What is it?"

"Nothing. Please rest. I'll be back soon." It was a gentle, unperturbed melody, and she lay back for a moment, staring at the ragged cirque rim. Then she was on her feet and moving quickly up the slope and through the entrance. There were voices coming from the camp area. She came swiftly down the sandy ramp and around the rocks, where she saw a group of seven M'dians standing in a loose semicircle around M'landan. On either side of him stood Tlaima and Klayon. Darenga came toward them at an angle, positioning herself where she could watch the movements of the newcomers.

They had seen her approach, and stopped their conversation. They looked at her with eyes shaded and dull.

You'd better fear me, she thought grimly, determined that she would not be sent away this time. She remained motionless, her hands on her hips.

"You come to ask help from one whose powers you have limited," M'landan said in his formal tones, apparently continuing where he had left off.

One of the females in the group, another weaver, replied, "We are grievously ashamed, my priest, for what we have done. We ask only that you forgive us, that you tell us if our gods forgive us, too."

M'landan stood silently, looking down at her. "Very well," he replied, "I will speak to each of you in turn. Gratene, come with me." Flanked by Tlaima and Klayon, he turned and walked to a small outcropping and sat down.

Gratene knelt and rested her hands on his knees as

Treaden had done. When M'landan began speaking to her in a low voice, Darenga kept her eyes on the other M'dians, who were watching the tableau at the rocks with only an occasional glance at her.

As far as she could make out from the fragments of drifted song, M'landan was asking Gratene much the same questions he had asked of Treaden. Then she heard him ask quite clearly, "And what of the one who stands apart from all of us?"

Darenga looked toward him, isolated suddenly by the meaning and tone of his song. Gratene's head turned.

"She has made us barren, my priest; there will be no generation to follow us."

She said more to him in answer, but she had looked back to him and her words were muffled by her hood. Darenga saw M'landan lean forward, heard his voice, but couldn't understand what he was telling her. Gratene rose then, drew her hood about her face. "May I stay?" Darenga heard her say. M'landan answered in the affirmative.

She had not been given absolution. Darenga watched as she moved slowly away to the edge of the camp area and sat down in the sand, her hands folded into her lap, her head bowed forward.

M'landan spoke to each M'dian, some of whom he denied, others of whom were given remission. All asked to stay, and he refused none of them.

He got up from the rock and stood for a moment with Klayon and Tlaima, the three hoods bent together in conversation. Then he broke away and came over to where Darenga waited.

"They wish to stay with us," he said. His voice was low and the notes were heavy. "The city is being split between those who follow Laatam and Trolon, and those who would seek their way back to the gods through me."

She was alarmed at how tired he sounded. "You need rest," she said. "You still haven't recovered."

"Yes, I know. I was going to lie down for a few minutes. And perhaps have something to eat? . . ."

"Of course. I'll get something for you."

When they were inside the cirque, M'landan dropped onto the cloak and lay back with a heavy sigh. "Everyone who will not proclaim against me is being sent away from Ilanu, and they're being denied their portions."

She held a bowl of congealed plovaan out to him. "That's a little savage, isn't it?"

He sat up and took the bowl, pressing the blunt end of the gauntlets against the sides. "Trolon and Laatam didn't know there were so many who would disagree with what they . . . helped bring about."

You, too, have difficulty ascribing blame, she thought. *Your demands on yourself are too harsh.*

"How many are there? Do you know? Will they all come here?"

"More are standing with Laatam and Trolon than are committing themselves to banishment. But there will be enough, there will be enough. We must limit our provisions; everything must be portioned."

Darenga leaned back on her heels and watched him extend the long, tubular tongue into the bowl. "For what duration?"

He looked up from the bowl, retracted his tongue. "For as long as the provisions last," he answered. "Tlaima and Klayon are determining what we have now, and then we can plan on what we are to do."

"Well," she said, getting to her feet, "at least I can help with that."

"Wait . . . please; there is something more I would speak with you about."

"Yes, what is it?" Her mind was already racing ahead, engaged in those things she was familiar with during uncertain times: supplies, rations, distribution.

"Please," he said, "please sit down." He maneuvered his bowl to one side, straightened to look at her as she seated herself crosslegged on the cloak in front of him.

"You're not eating," she told him.

"In a moment." He placed his gauntlets in his lap, sat very still. "Do you remember what I said to you before you fell asleep?"

She looked at him blankly. Then, "Yes, something about a ceremony, wasn't it? I'm sorry—I did fall asleep."

The moments before that conversation streamed back across her mind, and she saw that his memory had swiftly paced her own.

"A ceremony that would join us." He said it quietly enough, but his voice betrayed him.

"Shoma?"

"No, not shoma; there are too many restrictions; something else."

"Does it matter now? Is there anyone who isn't aware of our relationship?"

He didn't answer her directly. "There are reasons this should be done. My people must know that before this tragedy was worked on us our union was sanctioned."

"Sanctioned? By your gods, you mean."

"Yes, of course. My error was in not proclaiming it at once, to you as well as to my people. But there was . . . a lack of clarity . . . appeasements to be made. . . ." He explained no further, and Darenga asked him no questions, sensing in the few phrases a great reluctance uncharacteristic of him. A reluctance which seemed to disturb him to voice it.

"If you feel this is necessary——"

"Yes, I do. Even the Chaeya of a banished priest should have certain traditional rights."

"You're concerned for my safety," she said, finally hearing the tone that revealed his fear.

"I'm uneasy, yes."

"You don't have to be. No one—believe me—is going to hurt me, or you again."

He regarded her thoughtfully. "You are strong, and experienced in violent matters——" It was said objectively, with no hint of condemnation, but Darenga shrank inwardly. "You have commanded a great space ship, and the people of many worlds have been under your authority, but, against everything I thought possible, I saw my people strike you down, and I know they would have killed you in another moment——"

She shook her head. "No. They wouldn't have killed me. I could have taken you out of there."

"I feared for my people, too."

In his song there was more than the meaning conveyed by his words. He had known what she was capable of doing even without weapons. And he had been made horrifyingly aware of what his people were capable of. Buried in their quiet tolerance was behavior he had never experienced, instincts unloosed which had been lying dormant for thousands of years. When he had commanded her to go, he had not been sure if she could make it through the city alive. She was incredibly strong and disciplined for violence, but the sheer numbers of his people and the intensity of their purpose would have brought her down if they had pursued her. And she would have killed many before she died. And there would have been no recourse to the gods for any of them.

He sat looking at her from the shadow of his hood. She was always fire; it ran along inside her, directing her movements, guiding her thoughts, the same fire that had driven her species to the stars. And he could hear that burning. He knew when she was angry, when she was tired, when she was frightened, when she was close to tears. And he knew it in spite of the strange rigid control she imposed on herself.

He could see her burning. The eyes that had been evolved by his ancestors, deep in the endless twilight of the caverns, saw in ranges far beyond the human eye. Her radiation was visible, and he knew what its fluctuations meant as well as he knew his own. There was an intensity about her now as he waited for her response. It gradually diminished as he watched: her control again, managing fear. And he wondered what it was she feared.

"If you feel this is necessary, it's all right with me. But I don't know very much about this sort of thing. You'll have to explain it to me. Tell me what to do."

Acquiescence. So rare in her.

"I will have Tlaima and Klayon explain these matters to you. It would be more according to custom that way, and I think that to follow tradition as closely as possible would be the wisest course."

"I agree." She paused. "When will all this take place?"

"Soon," he answered, and did not elaborate.

After a moment, she rocked back on her heels, preparing to rise. "Well, maybe I should help Tlaima and Klayon now—"

"Areia," he interrupted quietly. "Would you be kind enough to . . ." and he glanced down at the bowl he had set aside.

"Of course. Gladly." She held it up for him, and he bent his head over it, his great eyes watching her solemnly all the while he siphoned the pale jelly from the bowl.

He doesn't want me to leave him; he's as captured by this feeling as I am, she thought, and it surprised and touched her that he had not shown this dependence before.

Or perhaps she had been so engrossed with her own inner change she simply hadn't noticed. But obvious at this moment was the fact that he was as vulnerable as she—vulnerable beyond the natural frailness of his body, the frailness she tended to overlook in the force of his personality. And she considered whether that strength would be enough. Events had caught them up and were rolling over them with the vast inevitability that such things did. Yet within all the horror and cataclysmic reversals he somehow had kept steady, unwavering, sure of each decision, of his own role in everything that had occurred. She acted on each event, responding to the event itself; he seemed to proceed from a broader sense of pattern, an intuitive grasp, an extrapolation of whatever present he was analyzing. It came, she realized, from a deep understanding of his people and his planet. And yet, that one time, he had been so blind and she had seen so clearly. Strange that he had been, in essence, abandoned by the summary of his life in that one instance.

He had finished, and now leaned back against the wall. "Would you like more?"

"No, thank you. I think I'll rest now." He tucked his arms into his sleeves, settled his shoulders against the rock.

She got up. "If you need me, just call."

He shook his hood further over his face and answered in a muffled voice, "Yes, I will."

She walked away then, and, as far as she could tell, he fell instantly to sleep.

The three of them stood around the rock shelves that held all the provisions—the jars and bowls, the bottles and tubular containers that stored the nourishment from L'M'dia. There were rows of hanj pods, and all the rolls of fabric, tools of one kind and another, all those provisions which represented the shares of Tlaima and Klayon.

"We can't parcel out our resources until we know how many will be with us," Klayon said.

"We have more of plovaan than anything else." Tlaima was shuffling through the jars, tipping them slightly, rolling them on their heavy ends into new positions as if that might increase their number.

"There's one thing that has to be done now," Darenga

told them in a low voice, "Take out a supply of lumeena for M'landan; put it out somewhere. Hide it where no one will find it."

"He would forbid—" Tlaima began.

"If you can't wrestle with your ethics, tell me how much he needs, and I'll take care of it."

"The thought is there, nevertheless, Areia," Klayon said. "And do you think we can lie to M'landan? Do you think we would not be instantly found out?"

"How much of this do you think he can take on the kind of rations you'll be on? He's still too weak. He hasn't recovered. Right now he's lying in the cirque, completely exhausted. And what the hell happens to all of you if he dies? How do you reach your gods then? You'd better take damn good care of your priest now, whether he wants it or not."

There was a little silence. Then Klayon replied, "We realize you suggest this out of love, but for us to do what we know he would oppose is impossible. He must be consulted."

"So he can say no, give it to the people? To the people who cut off his hands!"

They both stared at her. "You have so far to go!" Tlaima cried out in compassion.

"Don't give me that!" Darenga responded quick and hard. "I'll tolerate it from M'landan, but I don't want to hear it from either of you!"

She swung around, ran her hands over the jars on the shelf in front of her, settling on one large one and lifting it away. "At a vial at a time, one of these should last six months, anyway."

"Listen, please!" Klayon said, stepping forward, but not barring her way. "We can't stop you from doing this, and we know you have only the best intentions. But consider this: if M'landan saw the rest of us hungry, do you think he would take one drop, even from your hands?"

And she stood with the jar, like logic solidified, in her arms, her eyes locked on the dark circles that stared out from the hood.

"Are you going to let him die?" she said finally, her voice strained.

"Would you make a fool of him?" Tlaima said then,

coming up beside Klayon. "Would you take his dignity away by subterfuge? Let him know what you wish for him. Tell him. If he should decide it's right—what you suggest —then he will do it. But speak to him."

Darenga replaced the jar on the shelf and turned back to them. "I hope you know what you're doing, because if you don't, you're going to have a bitter load on your consciences."

The people began arriving before the end of sunfall, and with less than two hours' rest, M'landan came out to meet them. The atmosphere was different now; there was a desperation, an intensity that crowded into the gathering numbers like a physical presence. The people pressed in on M'landan, touched him, called out to him, pleaded for his attention. Darenga, seeing the aborted motions he made with his arms, realized that the powerful calming effect he had been able to produce had almost wholly resided in his hands. Or the combination of voice and hands; he was swinging far across his vocal range, wide into the upper and lower frequencies she couldn't detect except in the responses of the ones around him who showed some lessening of the tension in their manner whenever his voice faded out of her range. Within this mob, Tlaima and Klayon shifted about him, trying to act as a buffer, but there were too many.

"Please!" M'landan suddenly cried out. "Please, I will speak to you all. You must give me space; a place to sit down!"

Darenga was beside him in an instant, and this time he did not send her away.

"You come with us," she told the nearest M'dian, and to the rest, "You will have your turns. Go sit down, all of you!" And to Klayon and Tlaima, "Give them something to eat and drink and arrange some order for them to follow so they know they'll get a chance to speak with him."

She turned back to M'landan, who waited calmly now for her to guide him to the cirque. When she saw him seated comfortably in the chair, she leaned down to whisper, "Will you need Tlaima and Klayon?"

"No, not for this." She could hear the fatigue in his voice.

"Can I do something else for you?"

"No. Please ask Klomio to come forward, and then if you would stand at the entrance——"

"Of course," she answered, and thinking it would be best to get it over with as quickly as possible since he seemed determined to speak with them all, she motioned for Klomio, and then retreated up the slope.

But it was hours before the last M'dian rose from the sand in front of the chair and moved past Darenga and around the cirque wall toward the campsite. M'landan had remained seated, his gauntlets resting in his lap, his head bowed.

"You're exhausted," she said, laying back his hood and tilting his face up so she could see it. His face was drawn, his mouth tight, his eyes pewter globes that absorbed all light and held no image. "Will you lie down now? You have to rest——"

"Laatam has approached the priest of Klada," he said wearily. "Only twenty of my sisters will be allowed to conceive, and of those twenty, three may remain in Klada. The rest must bear their children in other cities."

"Why? Why can't they stay in Ilanu?"

"Ilanu has no priest. It is Protain's seed; he determines what is best for everyone, and this is his decision."

She would have said something further, but knew it would have upset him. Instead, she arranged the hood back around his face, lay her hand on his shoulder.

"Will you rest now?"

"Soon." He came slowly to his feet. "I want to see they've all found places, that they're comfortable."

"I can do that for you. And Klayon and Tlaima are out there giving them food and water. They're all being taken care of. Why don't you lie down and let me get you something to eat, it's been hours——"

"Your hands are warm and sweet," he told her softly. "Will you wait here for me?"

Gentle dismissal. "Yes," she said, stepping back. She watched him go slowly up to the entrance. She gave him time to clear the ramp, and then followed him, coming around the cirque to where she could look down on the campsite but still remain in the deep maroon shadow of the walls.

He had walked out among the figures crowded into the campsite. Most had made pallets and were either reclining on them or sitting with bowls in their hands talking quietly with one another as Klayon and Tlaima attended to their needs. Now, as M'landan entered their midst, they turned to him, ran their fingers along the hem of his robes, reached up to touch the gauntlets that hung down at his sides.

They're making him into a martyr, she thought. *That will be a deadly danger to Laatam and Trolon. He's got to leave this place for his own safety.*

As she watched, they crowded around him again, winding him with melodies that held him like a web. No one spoke his name anymore, nor used the more formal address "my priest." Now, spontaneously, they had renamed him L'Hlaadin, *Holy Guide,* the name sung in tremolo on a sliding note of sadness and tension that sank like mercury to the center of her heart.

His hood glinted above them as he turned his head down toward their faces, speaking first to one and then another as they clung to his arms, held his wrists up to their ear membranes. Each time he would gently disengage himself with a few murmured words.

Can't they see how tired he is?

Darenga would have gone down to him, but he had wanted her to stay at the cirque, and she obeyed with growing anxiety as the crowd showed no signs of letting him go. But finally there was an abrupt movement, and a pathway was opened from him to Tlaima and Klayon, who stood near the edge of the campsite. He joined them, and the M'dians returned to their pallets, looking after him until the three figures had walked out of their view.

Darenga retreated into the cirque and lay down on the cloak, waiting for him to appear in the entranceway. She judged the passing time by the slow wheeling of the star groups that glowed palely above the rocky rim, the universal clocks that tolled down the thick sky above her head and disappeared.

And still she waited and listened and heard nothing but the silent indication of sleep. Out in the campsite, the forgiven and the denied lay together and slept. She got up and paced the confines of the cirque, climbed to the entrance and swung away. He had been definite in his quiet way, and so she did not leave to search for him, but continued to pace in the balanced stride of a sand walker.

The pacing accomplished little, acting more as a winding mechanism for her anxiety than for relief. Finally, she lay down on the cloak, adjusted the folds of her robes, and closed her eyes.

He's all right. He will come soon. Her arms crossed slowly over her face.

Chapter 8

When she awoke at first sunfall, Tlaima and Klayon stood at her feet. She sat bolt upright. "Where's M'landan?"

"Near the spring."

"All this time? Is he all right?" She ran her fingers through her hair, twisting it into a quick heavy coil that she pulled over one shoulder and held as if it were a lifeline.

"There are certain private rituals he must observe to prepare himself for your joining," Tlaima said.

Darenga got up, sensitive instantly to what their voices might reveal. But they stolidly met her eyes, and Tlaima said, "We're to instruct you in this ceremony and what it will mean for you to be the Chaeya."

So soon. She sensed the urgency behind their appearance and M'landan's absence. Apparently he had reasoned as she had. "All right," she said slowly.

"First the ceremony," Klayon said, beginning in his methodical way. "It is not a shoma, but it will have the sanctity and commitment of true shoma. M'landan must both conduct and participate, so you will be facing him until he comes to your side. We will robe you, and offer you to him. At that time you will kneel. We will be on either side of you, and will make the proper responses—"

"—which is customary," Tlaima interjected. "You will have one response, and that will be your assent to this joining and all its obligations."

"What are the obligations? I'm sure there must be some that I can't physically carry out. How does that affect this ... bond? The legality of it, I mean."

"You're both limited physically," Klayon answered in a mild tone. "That is why M'landan has chosen this way to join you. The obligations are lifelong. From this time on

94

you will remain at his side except for those times he indicates you should stand away——"

"——you mean literally at his side?"

"Yes. It will be expected of you, and it would be humiliating for M'landan if you do not. For you to join with our priest is to fulfill him—*ana-il'ma*—" Klayon used a metaphor of L'M'dia, a device which so much of the language involved, and which meant to ripen or to fill the globe, *ana-il'ma.* "Our people will recognize it if you slight him."

"Your ways are very different from ours," Tlaima told her. "It will not be easy for you. The demands on him are growing, and he has had to meet them in new ways, outside our traditions. The situation now is . . . not as we've been trained to expect. We work in darkness and he is our eyes. . . ."

A sense of groping in a strange darkness for something familiar, she meant. *Well, I share that with them*, Darenga thought. She said, "I'll do whatever's necessary; whatever he wants me to do, for as long as I can." Then, shying away from the thoughts that stirred, she asked, "How will the people out there take this?"

"We . . . think it will be accepted."

"But you're not sure?"

Klayon answered, "They will have to."

Darenga was silent for a moment. "They're making him into something that may destroy him; am I to be part of that?"

"We don't know why this has happened," Klayon answered. "It is strange, to say the least, but M'landan says nothing about it. We think he may have known it would happen."

"Why do you say *destroy*, Areia?"

"Because he's drawing too many away from Ilanu, and Laatam and Trolon are being too severe with their edicts. The history of my world is bloody with this kind of righteous vengeance. I can tell you that they won't let it rest with trying to starve you out. What I'm afraid of is their spreading this into the other cities—stirring up a crusade against M'landan. That's why I asked you if this . . . joining won't intensify the anger and resentment already levelled on him."

"It would make no difference," Klayon said. "He has decided."

"And what about you," she asked them both, "do you resent me for this?"

"I do what my priest tells me to do," Klayon answered. "Although I think it's strange he would choose someone not of his species for his mate, I trust his judgment. If I were to resent you, I would be showing contempt for the gods, because you are guided by them as we are, through M'landan."

Darenga let that pass, and turned to Tlaima. "And you?" she said softly.

"He had chosen you long before this tragedy. I saw it in his manner and heard it in his words when he announced, that day in the gathering room, to prevent your being cast out of the city. It has weighed on him heavily for many years. You were slow in realizing it, Areia. He has done you a great honor, our maimed and suffering priest—" she began to cry, and there was from Klayon a swift compassionate vibrato. He looked anxiously at her, and then put his arm about her.

He loves her, Darenga suddenly realized. *He loves her, and she loves M'landan. What an abysmal mess.*

"*Mlo saindla!*" Tlaima was saying to Klayon. "I don't wish to torment you." Her hand pressed against his chest.

He answered her in a higher register not audible to Darenga, and Tlaima responded in kind, the gestures of her hands as revealing as her words would have been.

Presently they both turned back to her, and Tlaima said, "There is so much confusion for all of us."

They began again.

"There is the cleansing that we must perform," Tlaima told her. "And then you must be anointed. May we help you with your robe?"

After a thoughtful hesitation, Darenga allowed herself to be stripped by Tlaima and bathed by Klayon, who went about this task with surgical thoroughness that admitted only a slight professional curiosity.

"I see Yamth has touched you twice," he said matter-of-factly.

"What? . . . Oh," she replied.

They brought her a fresh robe, helped her fasten it. When she asked about the wide bronze band that had been added to the hood Klayon told her, "It was M'landan's instruction."

All at once she wanted to see him. "What else have we to do?" she asked.

"Only one thing more." Klayon went over to the chair and retrieved a small jar. He set it in his palm, lay his other hand over it in a practiced motion, and brought it to where Tlaima and Darenga were standing.

The jar was beautiful, inlaid with silver representations of L'M'dia and figures with banded hoods. It was old, extremely old, the silver bright and smooth with use.

"What's in it?" Darenga asked.

"Sacred oil. The virgin oil from the first pressings of L'M'dia. And it holds the first blessed laanva from our priest's hands."

He dipped his fingers into the jar, held them briefly suspended above it so no drop was wasted. "The oil is the blessing Yamth and Baandla have given us. It gathers in L'M'dia during the lifetime of a generation, and we use it to consecrate our most sacred rites. In shoma, it's the essence of fidelity and love."

He raised his hand toward her. "I will place it on your eyelids—"

Darenga stepped backwards. "I'm allergic to the plant, Klayon," she said, coming abruptly out of her trance-like contemplation of the jar which held the laanva from M'landan's palms. "It's poison to me. And the oil especially, because it's so readily absorbed. If it touches my skin it will enter my bloodstream. I can't have it on me."

Klayon drew his fingers back over the jar. "You don't have to be afraid; M'landan said the oil would not be harmful to you."

"I can't do it, Klayon. I'll die if it touches my skin."

"This is an important part of the rite of the shoma tradition; M'landan wants it preserved. His instructions must be followed, or this joining will not find perfect approval."

"Let me talk to him—"

"Do you think he would do anything to harm you? He said it would be safe for you. Trust him."

She held his eyes for a long moment, then glanced at Tlaima. "This would be the first obedience," she said, and Tlaima answered, "For perfect approval, there must be perfect trust."

"I do trust him." She turned to Klayon. "Go ahead."

97

"This is a rite you must perform on him, Areia. This is what you will do and say."

She closed her eyes to the glistening fingers, felt them press over her lids.

"*Pla mg tlo dimenan.*" My eyes will see only my beloved.

If I'm to die . . . If I'm to die now. . . .

Klayon's hand dipped to the jar, touched her throat. "*Pla slaam laa nomme.*" My voice will speak his name.

M'landan, if I'm to die now. . . .

His fingers traced the ridges of her ears. "*Laa som mg mlo gaedon.*" His song will guide me from this time on.

The oil was cool, scented with honey, soothing.

Every test run by the medical staff on her ship had indicated that the reaction to contact with the extracted oil of L'M'dia would be instantaneous and fatal. And yet he had said, *it will be safe.* She opened her eyes and found that Klayon had stepped away.

"I'll hold out the jar to you when it is time," he said. "Now we'll take you to him."

They started up the slope to the keyhole, Tlaima and Klayon falling slightly behind Darenga, then pacing her again as they turned down toward the campsite.

"You will approach him, and when we have presented you, you will kneel." Klayon was speaking rapidly now as they crossed the campsite.

"He will address the gods, ask for their blessing. Then he will tell you to rise, and he will take his place beside you."

They were passing through the lines of people who pressed aside as they drew near.

"I will hold the sacred oil out to you, and you will use the words I used."

She saw him then, standing beyond the people in the flutter of Baandla and the rusty light of steady Yamth, a solitary figure so familiar and at once so strange, as if a universal glass had slightly turned and the usual was somehow suddenly fantastic.

"He will ask you if you fully accept—" Klayon was still giving his low and breathless instructions "—the obligations of the union he proposes, and you will respond. . . ."

A blur of faces, and then the one face that in that one moment and circumstance was the one face in all time she could not touch. *Ah, M'landan, I come to you cleansed and anointed, in fresh garments and an attitude of mind I never thought I could have.*

They brought her in front of him, and then stepped to the side and behind her.

"I'm to kneel. . . ." She sank down, her eyes on that familiar-unfamiliar face.

"My Gods," he said then, "look into this shelter of darkness and reflection; see us as we ask thy blessing on the joining of thy servant and the one who has sought peace in the shadow of thy light."

He wasn't speaking in the clarion tones of invocation she had heard him use so often, but instead in an intense and intimate tone which revealed even more to her about his relationship with his gods.

"Thou hast looked deep into thy servant's heart, my Gods; and thou knowest, as thou knowest all things, what lies in the heart of the one who kneels before me. In all things her thoughts and her actions have been to shield thy servant in the general calamity. Her transgressions were committed in ignorance, mine in full knowledge.

"Thou hast always known what lies at my heart's center. O Gods. Thou hast guided my path even in this. Bless with your ever-flowing love, that reaches even into the stiffness of the proud mind, this joining of thy servant and the one who far-journeys."

He looked down at her, as he had been doing all the time he had been speaking. And then, slowly, as if he were giving it deep consideration as he was doing it, he knelt. There was a sudden breathless silence, and then a rustling of cloth as the gathering came to its knees. Darenga sensed a hesitancy around her. M'landan had done something totally unexpected even by Klayon and Tlaima.

He had not taken his eyes away from her face, but continued serenely to hold her gaze, the gold and white light from the suns slivering over the curved black surfaces.

Feeling a movement at her side, she glanced away to see the oil jar Klayon was holding out to her. She dipped her fingers in and then held them carefully, as she had seen Klayon do, so the excess would fall back into the jar. But the oil was thick and clung to her skin. She raised her hand to M'landan's face, and he closed his eyes.

When she touched him he trembled, and her own hand became unsteady.

"My eyes will see—" she began, and he softly joined in unison "—only my beloved."

She faltered, caught by the pure scintillation of his voice.

She smoothed her fingers along his throat, and felt its fine vibration as he said with her, "My voice will speak her name."

He lifted his head then, as she first stroked his ear membranes with the oil, then impulsively leaned forward to cup her hands against his head. As she started to make the final response, he moved slightly, and she remained silent, her hands still inside his hood.

"My beloved and I will go out into the islands. She will lay a pillow of scented grass beneath my head. Her hands will be sweet on my face. The golden globes of L'M'dia will bend over us, and the air will be a windsong through the fan-stalks. My beloved's voice will be as clear as the air at first sunfall, and her words will be the windsong."

The flute-like tone rode and spun in the stillness, caught, turned upward, hovered, hovered, then slid slowly, gliding down into a low tense note. "My beloved will you accept what I can offer, forsaking all the attachments that still hold you to your people and your world?"

He had changed everything he had originally planned, she could tell that from the utter stillness of the people about her. And he was revealing something to her now that she had never realized he had understood, for by attachments he meant the reason for her original demands on him, her desperate need to use hallucination against the shameful fear and loneliness, the loss of so much that had only just begun for her, and of the human who had stood a barrier to the nightmares of her soul.

He was unsure of her. Through everything, he had been unsure of her.

"There is no substance in dreams," she answered. "And memories fade. I have no people but those who accept me here, no world but the world you offer me. And I willingly do what you ask."

There was a fluctuation in the shine of his eyes, as if obsidian and lead had welled up from some internal source of unresolved emotion. She started to speak again, to reassure him, but there came suddenly a current that passed over the sound receptors in her ears, washing in a sensation of sound where there was none. She started, her eyes going wide. Deep in the hearing centers of her brain came another sensation, like silence audible, indescribably heavy and severe, like blinding light translated into sound where there were no equivalents, nothing to judge by.

She swung her head away from M'landan's swift alarm. No one in the kneeling crowd seemed disturbed, seemed at all to hear what she was hearing. "Can't you *hear it!*" she cried, and couldn't distinguish her own voice.

She reached out for M'landan; her hands fumbled along his throat, found it still. Then his arms came up under hers, and, as he pulled her erect, she saw the sudden flash of terrible joy in his face.

Around her the people were rising; she saw them as she lowered her head, swung it to the side, feeling M'landan's arm tighten around her as he guided her in some direction she blindly followed with wooden steps, her whole conscious focus now on the sensation that was not sound, the nerve impulses from her retinas that translated into sound, taste and smell regenerated, magnified into total sound that was not sound at all. It bombarded her, entered every pore, filled her.

Gradually there was a reduction, diminishment, until nothing remained but the slow sift of their footsteps in the sand, the rustle of their garments, the soft drumming of L'M'dia.

"Can you hear me now, Chaeya?" His arm rested so lightly around her she could scarcely feel its weight.

"Yes," she replied, still stunned and groping.

He guided her through the islands, helping her onto one where he sat her down in the shadows beneath the nodding globes of the plant. He seated himself in front of her, lay his gauntlets on her folded hands. She stared down at them.

He waited. It was several minutes before she finally looked up at him, then he drew the gauntlets back into his sleeves. "Isn't the simplest answer always the more likely?" he asked quietly. "Reasonable minds have agreed to that in all ages and in all worlds, haven't they?"

"There are answers that rely solely on faith," she replied. "Reason is . . . suspended."

"And the explanations arrived at through logic are more comfortable?"

"More so than mystical explanations." She looked at him, her head still lowered. "I was shaken by the experience," she told him. "I haven't had time to analyze it."

"Why must you analyze? My gods have honored us in a way that no priest and Chaeya have ever been honored before; and you have been honored above all my people. Now I know my path is right. I have been uncertain about it—"

He, uncertain of his decisions?

"In these recent times my gods have often been silent when I most needed guidance. I have made desperate prayers. . . . My people sometimes frighten me with their demands." He looked down. "I cannot always do what they ask, but they have only me to guide them."

"L'Hlaadin," she said softly, sensing his fragility. Her own explanations had risen so readily to her mind: she was not insensitive to a strong telepath, and it was possible M'landan possessed that ability. She had none herself, but it was not a mystical gift, certainly. And there was the possibility that the effects of toxins in her blood had stimulated the hearing centers of her brain. But nothing could be proved or disproved, nor was any purpose served by offering him solutions that could only increase his uncertainty.

"L'Hlaadin," she repeated. "They called you that, not because they'd been trained to it from birth, but because they recognized it themselves. You've done the right things. They trust you, as I do. And your gods haven't been silent. . . ."

Presently, he said, "I have loved you long, my Chaeya."

"I was so unaware of it, M'landan."

"But my love was in secret," he replied quickly, and she knew it was because he thought she might say something he would have to rebuke her for.

She said then, to relieve him of that anxiety, "Is it traditional for the priest and Chaeya to come to the islands?"

"No," he answered slowly, "it is something I've thought about for a long time."

She smiled at him then. "I think the idea is lovely. May I make a pillow for your head? May I pull the grass?"

"Yes," he answered to both questions, surprised and so obviously pleased.

He watched as she drew handfuls of the long, purple grass and laid them, like sheaves of grain, on the ground near the pale golden stalks of L'M'dia.

"Lay your head on your cushion of grass, my loving friend," she told him, and then came down beside him, lying on her side, her head resting on her hand as she looked at him.

"It is as I imagined it," he said, turning his head toward her. "But there is something else. . . ."

"Yes? What?" she answered lazily, suddenly at peace in this moment of eternal and golden afternoon.

"I know there has been a longing in you to have our bodies touch. I have thought that would be very pleasant—to lie together that way. Would you like that now?"

"Yes," she answered, short and clipped, suppressing the sudden flare that would be detected in her voice.

"If you would unfasten my robes. . . ." he said with a mild excitement in his song—that innocence and openness which had always characterized him.

His skin was fine and cool, smooth along the length of her body. "Ah," he sighed. "Is this cruel of me? Or is it what you desire?"

She shook her head. "Don't ask me to speak," she finally answered.

"I know it arouses you. Would you like me to—"

"No, not now." But all the instincts were there as she kissed his face and pulled him against her. And then, as abruptly as her desire for him had risen, it receded, ebbing from her body as she still held him in her arms, leaving a deep calm and tenderness that had no part in gratified passion.

She stroked his face, kissed the wide curving mouth. "You've always been so loving, so tolerant," she told him.

"What I am is my nature to be," he replied, "and comes from the grace of my gods, just as the things I see in you come through a grace that resides beyond my heavens."

The admission caught her unprepared, and with the intuition created by struggle and disaster across a thousand worlds she knew with certain dread that it would have far-reaching effects. "M'landan," she said, in the grip of that intuition, "do you realize the danger you're in?"

"Yes," he answered. "It changes nothing."

Chapter 9

For the most part, M'landan and Darenga, because of her obligation as Chaeya, stayed apart from the still-growing numbers of displaced M'dians who sought refuge in their small camp. He met each group alone, preferring Darenga to stay visible but removed as he spoke to them.

To her pleasure and relief, she saw Braunsi and Sklova in one of the groups that straggled in. When they had spoken to M'landan and had joined the sprawling crowd that spilled beyond the confines of the earlier campsite, she sent Klayon to bring them to her in the cirque.

They walked down the slope, looking about them as they came, and then focusing entirely on her and the band she wore on her hood as she came forward. "Hello, my old friends," she said warmly.

"We didn't know the affection you shared with our priest was so deep," Sklova said in surprise, and added, "Events have moved so fast."

"But a true affection," said Braunsi. "Everyone knows that."

"Yes, of course. I meant no offense to you, Captain— oh! *mlo saindla*, it's not Captain anymore. Chaeya, I mean." The inflections she gave the name made it punctilious, formal.

"There's no need for ceremony. We're still the friends we were in the klaamet. Have you been made comfortable? Have you had something to eat and drink?"

"Yes. We had picked out our spaces, and food was being brought to us when you called for us."

"Then I interrupted you. Well, go and eat and rest. We can talk later."

"Yes, of course," they said together. Then Braunsi, "We would like that."

She watched them disappear through the keyhole. They

had been ill at ease; no memory of the hours spent in the laundry could overcome their natural impulse toward deference, now that they realized her relationship with their priest and brother.

She turned away. Then from the entrance, a hesitant voice spoke. "Chaeya?"

It was Braunsi come again.

"Yes, come here," she replied.

He came toward her then, and she took his hands eagerly.

"We were so glad to find you both still lived," he sang, the notes all a jumble. "This terrible thing! This terrible thing! We were asleep when it happened. Everyone crying and running from the dormitory. I could not believe such a thing could be done. So grotesque! So cruel! To cut off our priest's hands!"

"But he's alive," she said with great urgency. "You must be thankful for that."

"They call him L'Hlaadin," he said. "And there is a difference in him; he walks in the regions above us, now. I am so ashamed we took so long to escape the city."

"Escape?" she echoed, the part of her that was not the Chaeya, instantly alert.

"We were all confused when Laatam and Trolon told us all about the . . . transgressions, and said our priest had been justly punished and banished with the one who had led him from his people. They told us Protain of Klada was going to provide the seed for our generations and would take care of our religious needs. When we began to ask questions, we were threatened with banishment without our portions. We'd seen many of our brothers and sisters driven out, and we had no idea where they were to go, although we had heard rumors that there was sanctuary in the Yarbeen. But this has been so long a place of death. . . ."

She pressed his hands gently in an effort to calm him. "When did you finally decide to leave?"

"We knew it was wrong to remain in Ilanu when it meant we gave our consent to the thing that had been done," he answered, looking down at their hands, "even though we had had no part in it. So, early this sunfall, we made our way into the islands and found that others were doing the same. Together we reached this place and—

blessed be the names of Yamth and Baandla!—our priest."
He glanced up at her with a return of his shy expression.
"And our good friend."

"Yes," she said warmly, "and you and Sklova are especially welcome."

She looked up then and saw M'landan standing in the doorway, unmoving, his face hidden in the shadow of his hood and his arms thrust deeply into the wide folds of his sleeves.

She released Braunsi's hands, and they both turned to face him. "M'landan," she said, "has Braunsi told you how he and Sklova managed—"

He made no sound, but swung around and back through the entrance.

"Oh!" Braunsi exclaimed on a wretched note.

Darenga stared at the place where M'landan had been. Then, abruptly, she turned, took Braunsi by the arm, and drew him along with her up the slope. "Go on to the campsite," she told him. "Have something to eat and get some rest. I'll take care of this. And don't worry."

She saw him around the cirque and stood watching as he went back down toward the crowd. M'landan had not gone that way.

She had known instantly when she saw him standing in the doorway that he was displeased, but she hadn't known why, and still didn't. She felt the anger rise against herself, and resolved immediately to set things right.

She went from the cirque and made a slow pass around the campsite, but didn't find him. Thinking he might have gone into the islands, she wandered among them for awhile, and then returned to the cirque.

What the hell did I do? she thought in frustration. *What etiquette did I breach, or humiliation did I cause him that evoked such a response?*

She sat down on the cloak, wrapped her arms around her legs, and rested her head against her knees.

Braunsi must have known. But if I try to talk with him now it might compound the error. Damn!

She raised her head then, thinking she would consult with Tlaima and Klayon, and found M'landan staring silently down at her.

"You must never hold another male's hands," he told

106

her coldly. And she understood at once that the violation had involved more than an innocent breach of custom that, under different conditions, he would have perceived as such and forgiven immediately with the gentle explanations she was used to.

She rose up and put her arms around him as she might have captured an exotic and legendary bird. She found him trembling, yielding, his head bowing slowly. The gesture brought her hands up to his ear membranes.

"You know it was done in innocence and thoughtlessness. *Mlo saindla*, my dear and loving friend, forgive me and your brother who may have understood but was trapped by his shyness and by me. He wouldn't willingly offend you. And you must know I wouldn't either."

"I know these things," he said, still trembling, still discordant.

She hesitated, engaged in his obvious misery, but not knowing how to alleviate it. "I love you, my friend," she said, her voice reaching out to him in a low melody. "You're the only one I want to touch as we've touched." She drew his rigid arms from his sleeves, folded her own arms over his, and pulled them tightly between her breasts, cupping her hands over the blunt ends of his gauntlets.

"These are mine," she said fiercely. "When you suffer because of them, I suffer too."

"I know. And I know you both were innocent of all that entered my mind when I saw your hands together. I don't like this shameful feeling; I don't like it."

"This is my fault; I should have realized how it might seem to you—" and before he could speak she added, "But you should know me better than to think what you did. And Braunsi! He's such a child!"

"He's the same age as I am."

"M'landan, you can't let your people see you upset like this."

He looked down at her. "Who is it that rebukes the priest?" he asked gravely.

"His Chaeya and friend," she replied.

"Then come, Chaeya and friend, which you surely are," he said, putting his arm around her. "Come and lie down with me. I want you to touch me, every part of me. I want your hands to purify me."

* * *

Darenga looked at Klayon from where she was sitting cross-legged on the cloak. "What do you do when the food runs out?" she asked.

"I don't know," he replied.

"Food isn't our only problem," Tlaima said. "They have nothing to do. And everyone is so crowded here. But no one wants to move away from L'Hlaadin's circle, and they all fear the Yarbeen."

"Well," Darenga said, "there were 298 people at my last count, and all our arrangements were temporary to begin with. I don't know how much longer we're going to be able to sustain this population."

It was third sunfall. M'landan, as he did more frequently now, had withdrawn to a quiet area beyond the spring, and the three of them had gravitated to one another out of their sleeplessness and concern.

"He will find a way for us," Tlaima said with perfect confidence.

Darenga was silent, assessing her own feelings about M'landan and what he might be able to accomplish. They had neither fish nor bread on M'dia. Nor was he a Merlin. Other agencies would have to be employed.

She sat up suddenly, then leapt from the ground with Tlaima and Klayon at the sound of an abrupt commotion that reached them from outside the cirque. She was first around the corner, saw M'landan standing within a wide semicircle of M'dians from the campsite, all facing four M'dians in pale green L'M'dia-figured robes. They were not from Ilanu. They stood close together, their arms at their sides, looking nervously from M'landan to the people who now surrounded them completely, and then to Treaden, the weaver, who stood at their head, talking excitedly to M'landan.

The crowd moved aside as she came up with Tlaima and Klayon in her wake. She stepped quietly to M'landan's side, and stood listening to Treaden and watching the newcomers.

They were from Klada, and they were frightened. Being but a few yards from them, she could see the subtle differences in their features: the slightly oval eyes that were a lighter shade than the Ilanuians, the contraction and dilation that suggested a pupil, the totally iridescent skin that sheened in rainbows like oil, the mouth shape that was narrower and straighter than that of the M'dians who encircled them. All the subtleties of inbreeding.

Treaden, it was being revealed, had been operating an underground escape route of sorts. Most of the people from Ilanu had been filtered through it except for a few, like Braunsi and Sklova, who had gotten out on their own. It was clear that Treaden was being viewed by the exiles as a kind of hero, and now he had assumed the same role with this small band of Kladaks. There was certainly a grandeur in his posture and gestures—not bravado, but confidence and decisiveness. At the inner edge of the circle, Darenga saw Braunsi staring at Treaden, his eyes bright and black.

The change has already begun. Disaster coming like the taste of salt air before a gale. And M'landan directly in the path. Darenga looked over at him, recognizing in his patient, listening attitude disapproval. Or uneasiness, or both.

Treaden had been recounting the extended visit of Laatam and her entourage in the haruund of Klada, the sympathetic and generous response she had gotten from Protain, his subsequent return visit and long stay as he performed the offices of priest for the people of Ilanu, the relationship that had begun to develop between Laatam and Protain, her return to Klada with Protain to finalize the arrangements which the priest had undertaken with the other cities for her. Every time Laatam had left Ilanu, the ruling triumvirate had exerted severe pressure on the people, forcing out the ones who had remained faithful to M'landan.

Now Protain had announced that Laatam would be his Chaeya, and that had created an outcry in his own city. This group which Treaden shepherded was the Kladak Greynin. They had watched the machinations of Laatam, seen through them, had tried to counsel their priest, and had been told not to interfere. Because of their continuing opposition, they had been forced out of Klada. Treaden, having his ear acutely tuned to the situation, as a member of Laatam's entourage, had managed to convince the Kladak Greynin that they should at least approach L'Hlaadin with the story of their misfortunes.

"We are all ruled by the gods," was his reasoning, "and what has been put in motion by the gods through our wretched priest will be made right again through him."

This was said with rather a bold flourish, and Darenga could see how the Kladaks could have been easily persuaded to follow Treaden. But M'landan had not been impressed. And now he spoke so everyone could hear.

"My brother has undertaken a great deal. Not only does he pride himself in solitary activities carried out under risk to himself and others, he feels he can speak for the gods *and* his priest."

It was a severe rebuke, the words conveying less of the censure which M'landan placed on Treaden's behavior than the pitch and timbre and strong deep melody rendering them. It put restraint on Darenga's own swift approval of the M'dian's resourcefulness. She was, after all, no longer part of a society that normally valued this sort of heroics. Still, she felt an empathy with Treaden, who was being so rapidly deflated by M'landan's remarks.

"L'Hlaadin!" Treaden cried in dismay. "I didn't mean—"

"Who ever does, but the person bent on evil?" M'landan told him quietly. "Yet evil can come from actions taken with intentions that have a double edge—the outward expression proclaiming goodly purpose, which in this case it would seem to do, and the inward expression which takes its own satisfaction for the ultimate reason. My brother is a fine weaver, and the praise he receives for the beauty and intricacy of his cloth is properly accepted by him. But he thinks to weave a new fabric out of intrigue and excitement and to work honor and acclaim for himself into the pattern. These motives can be as evil as the misuse of a harvest knife."

That is harsh, Darenga thought as she watched Treaden's obvious distress. *But M'landan is right. And Treaden has done a dangerous thing in bringing the Kladaks here.*

Treaden rushed forward and grasped M'landan's arms where he held them inside his sleeves and leaned against them. "L'Hlaadin," he said, looking up into his face, "I want only to serve you!"

"And you serve me by acting in secret and without my consent."

"There was not always time—"

"You don't even fool yourself, Treaden. Why do you try to fool me?"

"You forgave me—"

"The gods forgave you one thing; this is another."

As this exchange was going on, Darenga's attention was on the figures who had drawn closer, their eyes on M'landan.

"L'Hlaadin, what do you want me to do?"

"It is not what I want, Treaden. It's what you know is the proper and truthful action for you to take."

Treaden stared at him, then slowly backed away.

Then, and only then, did M'landan acknowledge the Kladaks. "You are not unwelcome here," he told them. "But you have defied your priest, who, no matter how you may view his decisions, is the one selected by our gods to guide your lives. There is nothing in all the teachings that says a priest must have as Chaeya a resident of his own city, or even of his species. . . ."

Darenga looked at him. *Do you still have to justify me?*

"You are the Greynin. That means you suggest and advise in matters secular; you are overstepping your responsibilities and showing serious contempt for the gods when you try to change your priest from the course he has chosen. Do you think your knowledge is greater than the gods, Leadrin?"

The Kladak who stood nearest M'landan spoke. "Are you going to turn us away, L'Hlaadin?"

"Do you evade a priest's question? Do you think your knowledge is greater than the gods?"

"I think a priest may make mistakes. Even though he speaks with the gods, he is not one himself, and he is susceptible to . . . influences."

The silence in the listeners was intense and concentrated. No one moved.

A strange remark for him to make to M'landan when he is seeking asylum, Darenga thought, extrapolating several possibilities for this behavior, all negative. She shifted closer to M'landan and slightly ahead of him.

"If that is the interpretation you give your priest's decisions, I wonder why you came here. Do all of you feel as Leadrin does?" he asked the other three, and Darenga knew then that he hadn't been trying to justify his relationship to her, but drawing out the true outlook of the Greynin.

When they had indicated their agreement with Leadrin, M'landan said, "I cannot help you. You are not ready to help yourselves. Go back to Klada and appeal to your priest to allow you to return, and then accept what he has decided, as you are meant to do."

M'landan pulled his arms from his sleeves and drew the circle above them before they could speak. They stared at the gauntlets, fell back, turned through the opening crowd, and disappeared into the islands.

M'landan said to Darenga in a voice only she could hear, "Where is Treaden?"

"He went away into the islands," she answered.

"They will all oppose me now. I don't know what problems that will cause ultimately. But there is sometimes only one course of action. . . ."

She looked up into the hood at the face she could see but dimly, more the reflected light from his eyes than any distinct feature. There had been that indecision again.

I don't know how to help you. I don't have the sensitivity or the physical capability to hear the subtleties of your voice, all the modulations that would tell me the source of your indecision.

She asked softly, "What can they do?"

He turned away saying, "Come with me," and his quiet command included Tlaima and Klayon as well.

They followed him back to the cirque, sat down with him on the sand.

"This place is no longer safe for us," he said. "We are going into the caverns."

There was a quick intake of breath from Tlaima, and M'landan leaned over to lay his gauntlet on her locked fingers. "There's nothing for you to fear, my sister. Nothing. The caverns sheltered and protected our people in the distant generations; they will be our refuge now."

"I will go, M'landan, if you command it." She wrapped her fingers around the gauntlets, and they sat in an ultrasonic communication which surrounded Darenga like an invisible cylinder, a cylinder reaching from the core of the planet to the universe beyond.

She looked away toward the keyhole, toward the stars, toward a ship that shot like a sunbeam through time and space— She turned back, startled, when M'landan's gauntlet touched her face.

"We will go ahead with most of the people, if you will stay and direct the transport of the food."

"Of course."

"They will be as hesitant as Tlaima," he seemed compelled to explain. "There will be less fear if we lead them in."

"I understand. Go ahead, I'll take care of the food."

"Perhaps you would like the cart—" He glanced at the chair.

"Yes, I can probably use it." She lay her hand on his shoulder. "Going to the caverns is a good idea." *Such an inadequate gesture. All I have to offer.*

His hood moved toward Klayon, and she removed her hand. "We will start right away; they must be settled before Leadrin can align himself with Laatam."

Klayon and Tlaima rose together, M'landan more slowly.

"I will see you soon?" he asked Darenga, who remained seated. And it struck her as a particularly wistful and odd question.

"As soon as possible. There shouldn't be any problems."

After they left, after M'landan had stood poised momentarily in the doorway looking back at her, and then—unsatisfied, it seemed to her—walked away with the others, she sat with her head in her hands.

Finally she got up, stood looking at the chair. Then she began folding the cloth that draped it until it was once more revealed a cart. She tilted it upright, started to pull it up the slope. When from inside her skull, from outside a zone of space that was all space came the sound which was no sound but a threshold of all sensory experience, the tripping point of all sensation, directionless, powerful, unguided. Her hands gripped the cart handles. In an instant it was gone. And she stared at the cirque wall, wondering if she had really experienced it at all.

When she brought the cart down into the campsite the M'dians were already beginning to move out into the Yarbeen; their pallets rolled under their arms. Somewhere in the lead was M'landan, but the rock outcroppings obscured any view she might have had of him.

She pulled the cart down to the storage area, took a count of the remaining jars. Seven. *My God*, she thought. *Seven.* And as she recounted, the overrolling wave of sensation swept her again, and when it had passed over she found herself clutching the rocky ledge, her nails scraping the surface.

"Chaeya, can I help you?" It was Braunsi, standing at her side, his cloth rolled up and limply held over his arm. His voice showed concern, restraint.

"No," she said, pushing away from the shelf. And then, "Yes. Find me seven who will carry these jars," she said.

When Braunsi returned he had seven M'dians with him who willingly accepted the responsibility for the jars. He stood waiting, looking at her as she sent the seven off down the trail.

She turned back to him, stared at him. "Will you do what I ask without question?" she finally said.

"I will be afraid, Chaeya," he answered. "But I will do it."

There was, on the shelf, a small vial of oil left. With extreme care she poured some of it on the cart wheels.

"These robes," Darenga said, "are a hindrance."

"What would you wear instead?" Braunsi asked softly.

"My uniform."

They were crouched in the islands at the edge of Ilanu, feeling the quiet of third sunfall descend on the haruund.

"Do you miss the life you had, Chaeya?"

She looked away from that earnest and open face toward the haruund. "I miss the freedom of movement my uniform gave me," she answered curtly. Then, "I think we can move safely now. We'll take the cart up around through the klaamet."

Braunsi, bewildered by her unexpected tone, asked timidly, "What if someone should see us?"

"We'll run like hell."

The klaamet was silent, cool.

"I miss this place," said Braunsi. "We were so happy here."

There was such a note of sadness in his voice that Darenga lowered the handles on the cart immediately and put her arm around him. "Everything changes, Braunsi, even in Ilanu. And if you're going to survive, you can't mourn what doesn't exist anymore." She drew back and held his shoulders. "You understand that, don't you?"

"Yes, I do."

"All right," she said, taking her hands away. "And now we have other things to think about."

"I haven't forgotten, Chaeya," he replied, sliding his hands into his sleeves.

"I know you haven't," she said, and turned to lift the cart handles from the floor. "You lead; I'll follow," she told him, and followed after him.

She had learned her way about the upper regions of the haruund, but since she couldn't eat the food products of L'M'dia, she hadn't been interested in the vast storage areas that lay beneath the complex. All M'dians, however, knew their plan, where each type of food from plovaan to lumeena was stored. Unerringly, Braunsi went through the maze of silent corridors through a broad archway and into the huge storage rooms.

Everything was orderly, easily accessible. They filled the cart to the top, and then lay Braunsi's pallet cloth over all.

"We'll go back the same way we came," Darenga said. She handled the cart. As heavily laden as it was, it was not easy to pull, and so Braunsi pushed from behind up the inclines. They were both winded when they finally reached the klaamet again.

"Damn! but I'm out of condition," Darenga panted, propping the handles on one of the washing tubs while she went to get a drink of water from one of the silver taps.

Braunsi followed her over and cupped his hands into the flowing water, extended his proboscis, and drank, as Darenga stood to one side, breathing deeply, her hands on her hips.

"Do we go back now?" Braunsi asked when he had finished another handful of water.

"If you're ready," she answered.

They left the klaamet, made their way back around the far side of the haruund, where Darenga stopped. "When we start down the incline, stay clear of the cart. I don't want you run over by the damn thing if it gets away."

"But you—"

"Don't worry about me. Just keep to the side. We've made it safely this far, I want to be sure we make it the rest of the way. All right, here we go."

They started down the hill, Darenga bracing against the weight behind her, easing the cart ahead as Braunsi paced her anxiously a few yards to her left.

As she had said, her robe was a hindrance, wrapping

about her ankles with every slow step she made down the incline, and she was concentrating on achieving a rhythm that would keep it from tripping her, while trying to hold the rim of the heavy cart at a steady pressure against her spine, when Braunsi said, "We'll have a feast," as much, she realized, to gauge the endurance which would register in her reply as anything else.

"Yes," she duly answered, "a feast. You'll have plovaan, and I'll have dried raspberry root."

It had almost been too simple, this sortie that had gained them so easily what they needed. A disappointment almost, that they hadn't been noticed at all. The further they got away from danger, the more bold Braunsi became, but she knew he was relieved. She had to admit to herself that she was at least as relieved as he was—probably more, because she knew that if there had been a confrontation there would have been bloodshed, for she would not permit the people depending on M'landan to starve.

They had reached the last grouping of islands and, with Braunsi beside her, Darenga drew the cart through into the open sandy area that joined the Yarbeen. From out of the shadow line, M'landan came forward and stood silently waiting for them as they cleared the last island.

"Chaeya . . . ?" said Braunsi faintly, and Darenga answered with a tone deep in her throat.

"I did not think you would do a thing like this, Areia," M'landan told her when she had halted the cart in front of him. "Has nothing I've said made an impact on you? Do you go the way of Treaden? Exposing my brother to danger as well as yourself? And for nothing. Leave the cart and come with me." He started to turn, was arrested by Darenga's voice.

"Leave it? You mean here?"

"Yes, leave it here. It does not belong to us. It is not ours."

She was astounded. "There are seven jars left in your food supply! Your people are going to starve! This cart is only a small amount of what Trolon owes them. Everything we brought is theirs—morally and legally."

"Leave it here," he said firmly.

She stared at him. Then she said, "This is stupid," and started forward with the cart.

"No, Chaeya, please," Braunsi said. "Do as he says. Leave it here, please."

"We've just hauled this thing twenty miles," she told him, and then demanded of M'landan, "Do you think I'm going to let Trolon have it when your people are going to starve without it?"

"You will leave it here where Trolon can find it," he replied. "Or you can carry it with you as you wish. I will not stop you. But no one will eat it."

"Are you telling me you won't let them eat it?" she asked angrily.

"I will not let them eat it." He turned his eyes to Braunsi and added, "nor would they want to."

"Oh, L'Hlaadin," Braunsi said anxiously, as if he had been waiting for M'landan's attention to fix on him. "I seem to be always out of your favor!"

"You are out of my favor in this."

Darenga looked at them both, and then laid the handles of the cart in the sand. "Have it your way."

"There is no other way," M'landan replied.

She was angry at this sudden and unexpected clash, this repudiation of her judgment and action, his refusal to agree with her. But she took her place at his side as he turned from where the cart rested in the sand, and, in the silence that he kept, she suddenly felt isolated and foolish.

They joined the rest of the people in the canyon that lay below the plateau where the cavern entrance was located. M'landan went to a gap in the side wall of the cliff and led the way up the steep narrow path to the plain. It was as Darenga remembered it—green, barren of everything but occasional rock outcroppings and meager vegetation, a vast wide plateau that stretched over caverns that were miles deep.

The walk had given her time to rejudge her reasons for her anger, and she reluctantly determined that it had stemmed from her expectations of approval from M'landan: his rejection had taken her completely by surprise. Still, even though she had been deeply humiliated, she realized that there had been codes once which she would have died before violating: she could do no less than honor his code.

They walked over ground familiar to them both, the straggling silent line of M'dians behind them, and she remembered another time equally as grim when she had strode along with him in the glitter and authority of her rank, an escort of Patrolmen from the Galaxy behind them, a commander intent on finding treachery at all costs. And it had cost—everything.

She glanced over at him, found the deep shadows of his hood turned on her.

"We will talk, Chaeya," he sang with a tenderness that made her ache. "We will talk about all the things that distress us both."

The entrance to the caverns was a round chamber twelve feet deep and nine feet in diameter, bone-white, lustrous. It had a covering camouflaged to look like the terrain, but she had thrown it back years before, and it had never been closed again. Inside was a wide opening into the darkness that led underground.

She and M'landan went down first into the chamber, she treading down the chain ladder she had ordered placed there so long ago, M'landan floating down in a flutter of robes and landing lightly on the floor. The cool air from within the cavern circulated around them, carrying with it a faint damp odor that was pleasant and familiar.

One by one, the M'dians came down, moving out hesitantly but obediently after M'landan into the dark passageway beyond the chamber. Darenga waited until thirty or forty people had passed her, then, leaving the rest to be guided by Klayon and Tlaima, entered the passageway herself.

Unlike the eyes of the M'dians, which were adapted to—had evolved from—this environment, her eyes slowly adjusted to the darkness, to the vague shapes that marched silently downwards into the recesses of the planet. She began to make out some of the faces that glanced toward her as she went by. She read fear and anxiety and resignation on those features that flickered past in the cold, soft glow from the walls, and she turned aside for one, speaking gently.

"Atin, why are you crying?"

He looked at her, startled. "I have no idea where I am going, Chaeya, except that it is away from the light and my home."

"The light of Yamth and Baandla shine through your priest, Atin. That is your blessing in the choice you made to follow him. No one in Ilanu will have that comfort. You have much more than those you are leaving behind you. And, Atin, you're coming home; not leaving it."

"Ah, look!" came a soft cry, and the M'dians nearest to Darenga, and Darenga herself, looked out into a vast, pillared chamber that arched away to a distant ceiling that glowed like cloudy moonlight.

They moved on more slowly, turning their heads about to look up, to look around as they measured the columns that stood in groves, like slender saplings, or solitary, like massive redwoods, striated with age and strength, reaching up into the gothic stillness toward the far cold light of the ceiling.

Still on the descent, the train of exiles wound down through the pillars, M'landan at the head, his bronze hood glinting needles of fire as he led his people into the immense cavern.

It was through the last huge stand of pillars that the dwellings became visible, the enormous complex that had been carved, thousands of years before, from the soft native stone, and shaped into rounded clusters linked with airy bridges in a random sequence that reached from the deep floor of the cavern to the distant roof, and all bathed in the pale cold light that blanched planes and threw angles into black shadow.

The first of the line had stopped, and, as the others arrived, they fanned out in front of the complex. M'landan and Tlaima and Klayon stood facing them. Darenga, in the crowd, heard a soft lilting phrase quickly sung: M'landan's call to her; everyone knew it, that special fragment, and moved aside to let her pass. She took her place at his side, standing with her arms folded into her sleeves as she looked out at the hollow hoods that waited to be filled, to be activated, to be made less afraid.

M'landan began a prayer. She listened to his voice, not the words, because it was the rise and fall of the solemn baritone, close and resonant, that settled over her own nameless and gnawing fears. When the prayer was ended, Klayon and Tlaima directed the storage of the jars, and M'landan took for himself the task of settling the M'dians into the dwellings.

"We will take this one," he had told her before he left, pointing out a cluster on the second level that jutted out

119

from the rest of the complex like the prow of a sailing ship.

"You'd make a good commander," she had commented drily.

"Common sense, I think," he replied.

"It's a military position, my friend, not the position of piety and innocence."

"What a picture you have of me!" he had answered, and then left her to consider what he had meant by it.

The cluster he had chosen had four rooms, the room they would occupy standing forward from the rest but connected by a short hallway to two side rooms, which Tlaima and Klayon would live in. Beyond those rooms, the hallway opened into a larger common room that would, she supposed, be used as a sort of chapel.

She went back through the rooms and began clearing out the centuries' fall of rubble from the smooth floors and the ledges. At one point, Klayon suddenly appeared to hand over her cloak and look quickly around.

"It seems adequate," he pronounced, "and less frightening than I thought it would be."

"No, it's not frightening at all."

"If we must be exiles," he replied, "it's good that we come to the place of our origins."

"Yes," she said, looking away from him to the broad window opening that looked out on a forest of moonlit columns, "yes."

Chapter 10

She sat on the ledge with her back against the rock frame of the window. There were ghosts here, vague and trembling, wisps of body and posture, a pair of legs extended casually, ankles crossed, a voice indeterminate, a head turning, a word, a name, everything indistinct and evaporating, dissipating into the now, where many voices lilted and floated in a pure stream of sound so lovely it stung her eyes.

This is what I am; part ghost, part listener, an unwilling fraud on one who needed to believe and who saw mystic answers in explainable events, if I had only had the instruments to show it.

She leaned forward, her hands clasped on her knees. Then her head sank down, the copper hair tumbling forward out of the hood.

I can only receive when I want to give.

When M'landan came down from the complex, he found Darenga sitting cross-legged and placid on the cloak. She rose when he entered and stood watching him, her hands at her sides.

He had early learned that while that particular posture was, in his species, a sign of agitation and anxiety, in hers it was a gesture of composure. Only when the arms extended slightly from the body and the fingers curved inward was it a stance to reevaluate. She had not taken it often, but when she had there had been violence. Or the threat of violence. She was to be feared: he had seen that reaction among her own people. But he could see what they could not: her own fear and uncertainty, the radiant need that had been smothered by the ill-use of her society, the ill-use that even now filled him with the compassionate need to understand. But there was more than compassion; he loved her beyond any possible measure.

"Well," she said in the faintly mocking tone that always devastated him, "did you get the troops billeted?"

"Everyone seems comfortable and ready to rest." He sat on the ledge and gazed up at her. "Atin told me of your conversation with him. What was it you said now? Ah, yes; you said that the light of Yamth and Baandla shines through his priest and that that was the blessing he received for having chosen to follow him. A very pious and Chaeya-like remark for one who doesn't believe in such things."

She retreated into the sleeves of her robe. "He was frightened. I said what seemed appropriate."

He made a speculative tone, leaned back comfortably against the wall. "You often do," he said mildly. "How is it you know us so well and are only just learning about yourself?"

She sighed, and walked over to push back his hood. "If I'm going to spar with you," she said, sitting down beside him, "I want to see your face."

That, of course, ended it, because once he had turned his great eyes on her and gave her his whimsical smile, there was no more to be said.

"Are you hungry?" she asked, stroking his throat with the back of her hand.

"Very. And thirsty, too. Did Klayon bring in the container?"

"I don't know. He was here. I'll go check."

She got up and went into the hallway, glancing into the first side room as she walked along, finding it empty, and then proceeded the few meters to the second room and entered it. She stopped in her tracks. At the edge of the room away from the window, but touched with the light from outside, stood Tlaima and Klayon, rigid and unmoving, their hands locked together.

With a guttural oath, Darenga backed away, took a few steps down the corridor, and then was filled with a sudden blinding and inexplicable rage that held her to the spot.

"What is it?" M'landan said from the doorway to their room. "What's happened?"

Klayon spoke from behind her. "We were in communion when she entered the room, L'Hlaadin," he said.

"The water container, please, Klayon," M'landan said, coming forward.

122

"Yes, L'Hlaadin."

"If I touch you, will it make your anger worse?" he asked her gently.

"I'm not a wild animal," she answered fiercely. "I won't attack you."

"I wasn't afraid, Areia," he replied as she stalked past him. "I was unsure of the propriety. . . ."

Now there was humiliation as well as the self-directed anger that he saw revealed in her radiation pattern. As Klayon brought up the water M'landan held out his arm and gave him a gentle command in a high frequency. Klayon slipped the bail over his gauntlet and walked back down the hallway to where Tlaima stood waiting for him.

M'landan set down the water container, estimating Darenga's swiftly moderating temper as she stared fixedly out the window opening at the pale and silent columns. He started to speak, decided against it, and sat down on the cloak.

The anger was under control now, but the humiliation still glowed. Abruptly she turned and went through the door and back up the hallway. M'landan sat calm and still, listening to the quiet apology Darenga was making in the room down the hall. It was not easy for her, because of the unjust reason for her anger. But he considered that it was from such humiliations and acknowledgments that understanding would come for her, and, with the understanding, the peace she longed for.

M'landan was sitting with his eyes closed when Darenga came back. She sat down in front of him, and he opened his eyes and watched silently as she poured a bowl of water for him.

"Thank you," he said, but made no move to take the bowl himself, so she held it for him.

"Klayon is getting something for you to eat," she said as he drank in long delicate sips until the bowl was empty. By that time Klayon had brought another bowl which he left beside Darenga.

M'landan had finished half the bowl of plovaan when Darenga broke the silence to ask, "Why don't you tell me when you're hungry and thirsty?"

He drew up his tongue and sat back to look at her. "I forget. Until you remind me. Although I'm sometimes quite aware of my thirst."

"This, I suppose, is one of the main responsibilities of a Chaeya; keeping the priest from dropping over from starvation."

"My Chaeya, anyway."

She gave him a quick smile. "Yes, your Chaeya."

"Have *you* had anything to eat?" he asked, settling back against the wall.

"Well, no, I haven't. But you still have half a bowl left."

"I'll finish it in a little while." He watched her fumble into the pocket of her robe and finally pull out a cloth. She unwrapped and held up a squashed cube of dried raspberry root. "I guess I'm going to have to do some foraging next sunfall; this is all I have left."

She broke it in half and held one piece over for him to smell. "Ah," he said, "I like the fragrance."

"I know," she replied, and nibbled a corner off one of the pieces and sat chewing it.

"I would like to have seen your world," he said, after a thoughtful moment.

"Actually, I had two worlds," she told him. "Earth, my homeworld, and the Galaxies I've commanded." She gave him a quick intense look. "The Galaxy is what you should have seen. You were only on the bridge that one time—"

"I've never forgotten it! To see my own lovely planet as the gods must see it— Ah, Areia, you've brought me so much!"

She sat motionless. "M'landan. . . ." She faltered. "M'landan, whatever I've done that you find good is incidental—incidental to the time and the circumstances. None of it was initiated for your particular benefit. Just the opposite, in fact—" She held up her hand. "Don't reprimand me; I know what I'm saying is true. It's a preamble," she added, lowering her hand to her lap. "A preamble. You see in me what you want to see. Superficial things, some of them: you're fascinated by my hair, for instance, because you associate it with Yamth. You admire my strength, which, of course, is not unusual in my species and with the special training I've had. You remember the panoply that surrounds a Galaxy command. And—I don't know— because of a youthful indiscretion, you've imprinted me on your . . . psyche. Perhaps that's the ultimate answer for all this—"

"What question are you asking yourself? And me?" he interrupted gently.

She looked away. "I love you, M'landan—" a quick note came from his throat, making her hesitate, but he made no further sound, and she went on "—but I have no way to show it. I can do what is expected of a Chaeya; what I think that would be, try to anticipate you, but it's a duty I perform; willingly, you must understand, but still a duty that I carry out like so many others. The one thing I *give* you, the one loving act I perform for you, is to feed you, and even that is something you can do for yourself."

She stared down at her fingers spreading absently over the bronze cloth. "This is all very foolish and inconsequential, and I'm not dissatisfied. It's just that I have so little time left with you and nothing I can do for you but act out a role."

When she finally looked up, tilting her head slightly to receive a response from him, he said, "These are not foolish things, and I don't view what you mentioned as superficialities; I don't see them in isolation. . . ." He paused, his eyes on her face. "You see me afraid to answer. I'm . . . deeply affected by what you are trying to express. But I must risk your withdrawal by telling you that a heart to both receive and give love must first be cleansed of pride."

She looked down again at her hands. "Go on," she said.

"If you want me to."

"Yes."

"Your pride runs in many directions, my beloved. It precipitates your anger and your violence, and it demands defense of the life you were trained for, while not admitting the truth: that you were put to a selfish use by the leaders of your society. It prevents you from accepting what you have said you want, the thing you would be freely able to give, not just to me, for love is not a quality that can be limited."

"You won't see often what you saw happen in the hallway; I usually keep myself under control."

"Ah, but controlling pride isn't the answer. You must cast it away from you."

"I say anger, you say pride."

"What is anger but the manifestation of pride?"

"Perhaps anger is all I have left," she said, twisting the words bitterly.

"You must decide," he responded slowly, "what is more important to you. If you cannot relinquish your pride, you will never realize what is it you say you want."

She looked across at him. "And where do I begin?" she said, attempting sarcasm but failing.

"I will help you any way I can."

"I'm so fragmented . . . I wasn't always this way—"

"Pride, again."

"I can't believe in your gods, M'landan!" Harsh and sharp.

He moved his head slightly. "I have never asked you to," he replied. "I would never ask you to."

M'landan sat up carefully so he wouldn't disturb the woman who lay sleeping beside him, face down, her arms curved under her body so that her hands were hidden by the folds of her robe. Her breathing was relaxed and even, and her body radiation low and steady. He braced his gauntlets on the cloak beside her and bent over to brush his mouth against the explosion of gleaming hair that surrounded her face and shoulders. Then he straightened back around and leaned forward, drew into himself with his head deeply bowed. For a brief moment he was an image darkly carved, then his head lifted, and he cried out in a frequency no ear could detect, "My Gods, my Gods, give me guidance. Help me to see the movement I sense behind thy light. Allow me to hear the voice that speaks to me from beyond thy spheres. The words are indistinct and the sound confuses me. I have been obedient in all thy will has directed. Guide me now, I pray."

In the sunlight beyond the wavering shadow line, Darenga's robe lay stretched on the green sand. On it were thin slabs of raspberry root and one or two other varieties of M'dian vegetation, drying. Darenga herself, in the sleeveless inner lining of the robe, sat near a small campfire within the Yarbeen, looking at M'landan, who sat some yards away on a rock in extreme discomfort. The odor of roasting meat drifted with the smoke from the fire.

Darenga placed the skewer full of meat she had been holding on a little cairn of rocks she had stacked on the ground alongside the fire. "I can't do it, M'landan. I can't eat this while you're sitting there ready to throw up."

"Please," he said, collapsing his arms into his lap in a gesture of determination, "this is part of your existence; it is as much a function of your life as your breathing is. I must . . . must—"

"—endure it at all costs? The good with the bad, and all that? You know, I only eat these things because I have to. Ordinarily I rarely eat meat; although that's probably no consolation."

She stood up, shaking her head at him. "This is one thing I can't accommodate you in; I can't eat this while you're watching me."

"Oh, . . ." he began in frustration, and for a wild and funny moment she thought he was going to swear. And the thought so tickled her that she began to laugh. He gave her a quizzical look, and as she started to walk over to him, she suddenly faltered, came to a stop with a little cry.

"M'landan!"

She swung her head in rapid, abortive motions as if she were having trouble focusing on him. She stumbled, flung her hands up and mashed them against her temples. "M'landan!"

He jumped to his feet as he saw the brilliant fluctuation, the cobalt light stream out from her body.

"*M'landan!*"

"Yes, I'm here."

"Help me," she cried, reaching out. "I'm burning!" But when she saw him coming, she suddenly yelled, "No, *don't! Don't touch me!*" But he swam toward her through the waves of heat and rippling luminescence that his eyes saw radiating from her, his arms opening, the great wide wings folding around her as his scream ripped up through the audible range and beyond, continuing silently through the twisted slit of his mouth. His head arched back, exposing the vibrating throat. She had no strength to break the grip he had on her, so she stood helpless, numb as his scream went on and on.

Abruptly, his head snapped forward and struck her cheekbone so hard she staggered and gasped in pain. She was holding him then, too dazed to do more than let him sink to the ground, and she with him.

"Are you all right?" she asked. "Are you all right? Please, M'landan!"

"Yes," he answered, pulling her tightly against him. "I

hear you." His gauntlet was close around her neck, tugging her hair back. In a low, urgent tone he said, "You must never speak of this to anyone. Do you understand? No one must know about this."

She nodded, brought her hands up to his face, holding it so his huge eyes were fixed on hers. "What caused it? What was it? What's happened to us?"

"Tell me what you felt," he said with such intensity that she was immediately afraid to answer. But he asked again, and she said, "I was burning . . . I felt fear—for you. I thought. . . ." She was silent.

"You have no explanations, Chaeya?" he said, trembling.

"No, M'landan, I don't."

"Then I will give you one. *Ana-il'ma*. It was *Ana-il'ma*. The glorious light that poured from you has filled me—" he began to cry, bending forward into her hands. "You felt such a need to give, and what you have given me has altered us both."

He pressed his face against her hands, touched her palms with a quick stab of his tongue. "Beloved Far-journeyer, who holds the Globe and the Stalk, we are not to live out our lives on this planet."

They returned to the caverns, went quietly to their room. It was past third sunfall. On the ledge was a portion of plovaan and lumeena and a fresh container of water.

"I am more tired than hungry," M'landan sang softly.

She nodded and poured water into his bowl, and then knelt on the cloak beside him and took a drink. When she held the bowl out for him, he slowly came up on one elbow, staring at her silently before he drank briefly and raised his head again.

"Wait," he told her as she started to draw back the bowl. "You have shared common water with the priest from his bowl; now you will share something more," and he drew the blessing above the bowl. "Now drink again," he told her, and she obeyed, holding the bowl in both hands.

He drank once more, then, his eyes on her. "You must finish it," he said. "Water that has been blessed must be consumed."

It was a strange press of ritual and emotion that effected the difference. What had been water *had* become more than water by the fact of his blessing it and their sharing it, for in his lifetime no one had drunk or eaten from the same vessel he had. She had made this demand for acknowledgement in this suddenly heightened and closer relationship, and, swept up by this claim on him, he had yielded and then made his own demand. And she had not refused.

Chapter 11

Life in the underground city was calmer and less anxious than under the conditions that had existed at the campsite. A routine had been established, and the skills that had lain dormant during the first part of their exile were now being put to use by the Ilanuians. A water system was being set up in the complex, using an upper level spring that had been diverted away from the dwellings thousands of years before.

Braunsi and Sklova were already providing their particular service in a curious arrangement of pits they had directed to be carved out of the soft stone, pits which, on a graduated level with water flowing through, performed the same function as the tubs of the klaamet.

The weavers had put together crude looms from materials they had rummaged from about the cavern, trash thousands of years old and more recent. But as crude as they were, the looms produced, from the first experimental fibers made from Yarbeen plants, materials intricate and lovely.

What concerned the weavers, however, was tensile strength, and Darenga was called in frequently to test each fabric. Each time she managed to rip or shred or wrench apart the material everyone was disappointed, so disappointed that she was sorely tempted to resort to pretense, but she didn't, and the weavers continued to search for stronger fibers.

There were other projects, and Darenga was involved in them in the same general capacity she always was, until she began to privately refer to herself as the *trammelmare*, that particular beast of burden of the planet Arcus, a reptilian-mammalian type of creature, the female of the species being several sizes larger than the male and the one used as a draft animal by the Arcustans.

She had spent considerable time investigating her own motives and reactions to this role of strong woman, and found she simply felt exhilarated when she was approached to do anything, finally deciding that it seemed part of her niche in this society, and letting it go at that.

M'landan made no comment on her activities. He seemed, in fact, remote from the general busyness, leaving the planning and details to her and Tlaima and Klayon.

Although they had talked about their experience, all M'landan was able to tell her about the enigmatic statement he had made afterward was that he had "seen" them leaving the planet in an event ordained by his gods. As for the blue radiance he had described coming from her, she believed she had a reasonable answer: if he could perceive the heat flow from her body, perhaps her sudden physical pain had created a pattern he had perceived as well, and that, in combination with his strong emotional reaction, generated the state of mind which had extrapolated an impossible journey. But she knew the interpretation would have to remain a private one, because she also knew M'landan would never accept it. So, on that issue, she stayed silent.

He was preoccupied, and spent long hours away from the complex. But one sunfall she was helping to repair a structure just beneath one end of a bridge, trying to maneuver a large stone block into place, all sweaty, her sleeves rolled back, swearing with good humor as she tried to wedge the stone into the wall, when a change in the attitude of the M'dians around her caused her to look up. On the bridge stood M'landan, looking down at her with such an expression of love on his face that she promptly lay the block on the ground and walked the few steps to where he was standing on the arch. In the sudden quiet she lifted the hem of his robe and held it to her lips. Then she let it fall and raised her head to him.

"Oh, my Chaeya," he said, in a voice soft with surprise.

For a moment he seemed perplexed, as he glanced around at the upturned faces, and she addressed him, "L'Hlaadin, please come down. Let us show you what we've been doing. . . ."

And he did as she asked, standing near while she began the explanation of the structural problems they had had to contend with. The members of the repair crew soon added their comments with enthusiasm and appropriate satisfaction in what they had accomplished, while M'landan listened with the full attention he always gave anyone speaking to him. Yet Darenga sensed the division in his concentration, once the moment of confusion she had created with the humility of her gesture to him had passed. She knew he was attempting to focus on some future point, and the effort demanded all his energy.

Although his visit seemed unhurried, and his manner with both her and the crew gracious and interested, he was there and gone in a matter of minutes.

But he came in to her that same sunfall, after an absence of several sunfalls from their bed, and sat down beside her.

"You haven't eaten," she said, rising up.

"I've had no desire for food."

"Will you eat now?"

"Later, perhaps. I would like to rest first."

She put her arms around him, laying back his hood so his face was visible to her in the pale light from the window opening. "You look so tired, my friend. Can't I share any of this with you?"

"When you can," he answered gently, "you will know it." Then, curiously, he averted his face. "You will have decisions of your own to make," he said. "I pray they will not come to you too soon."

When he awoke, Darenga came forward, from where she had been sitting on the ledge, and gave him water and insisted that he have at least half a bowl of plovaan before Tlaima and Klayon came in to bathe him.

When all this had been accomplished, M'landan indicated that Darenga was to follow him, and they went out through the complex which was busy now and noisy with the first sunfall work. They left the complex, hearing fading behind them the song fragments and quick melodic jokes that showered down unrelated as they walked out into the pillars. Almost immediately the sound diminished and evaporated in the natural insulation of stone and form.

He walked beside her up the long, steep passageway, glancing over at her now and then, but saying nothing until they had come out of the entrance chamber and stood together in the maroon twilight of the Yarbeen.

"I'm going to Klada," he said.

"To Klada! Why?"

"We will need food. I'm going to speak with Protain. He should not be unsympathetic to our people. If the cities join, as I believe they will, then there will be an abundance. If Laatam is continuing unwilling to give us our portions, then Protain, I would think, would provide us from Klada's stores."

"But you don't know for sure."

"I believe he will respond in this manner. There is no reason why he wouldn't. He would not deliberately allow Laatam's people to starve. He would see there is no justice in that."

"Then why hasn't he done something already? He must know how we're situated. Surely the Greynin reported that back to him."

"Probably. But he can do nothing unless he is asked."

"No!" she replied, with such force that he turned all the way around to face her. "It's too dangerous."

"*I am going to Klada*," he repeated.

"I can't let you do that—not with the influence that Laatam has over Protain, and probably the Greynin, too. I won't let you go alone."

"You will stay here," he answered. "There is something you must understand, Areia. I have a course to follow, and I have to make my way along it without violence done on my behalf. I know I am your concern, that at this point in your life you have committed yourself to me. But it is absolutely forbidden that violence be used to protect me. This is the way it must be. And violence would surely occur if you were to come with me. Be obedient to me in this. Please trust me as you have been trusting me, for I can only suggest your path. You have it in your power to be either an instrument of deliverance or destruction, and what power I have is neutralized in the bond between us. I can't force you to take the right path, but I urge you to do as I ask. Stay here. I will be back."

She paced away from him, stood in profile, her face toward the city that lay far down the Yarbeen. "It's eighty miles," she said in a tight and grating song.

"I know the distance."

"You can't get food for yourself, or water from a container."

"There are springs between here and Klada, and I won't starve in the time it takes to make the journey."

He spoke softly, responding as she required, but she knew he was adamant, that he was waiting until she had adjusted to the fact that he was going.

"May I go with you part of the way?"

"It would be better to say goodbye here."

"There is more to this than you're saying." She paused, suddenly breathless. "We are joined by all the laws of your people and your gods, and yet you are silent about so much. Why?"

"You are not ready yet."

"Not ready," she echoed. "What do I have to do to be *ready?* What initiation do I have to pass to be able to share my husband's burdens—" She stopped abruptly and took a deep breath that outlined the bones at the base of her throat.

"You . . . you do to the extent that you can. What is not believed cannot be shared."

"What is this!" she exclaimed. "You cry out one moment that I've given you some mystical insight through gods I've never acknowledged—acknowledged! that I know to their last molecule!—and for this mystical gift I'm chastised by you; you equivocate and withdraw. This is insanity, to go alone to Klada! You're asking to be murdered! Do you think Laatam is so docile that she would allow Protain to do for you what she's turned Ilanu upside down to prevent?"

"Please!" he cried, turning his head from side to side.

She flung her arms around him, holding his head against hers. "Let me go with you! Let me protect you!"

"Oh, this turmoil! My Gods!"

She buried her head against his throat. "Cry to *me;* let *me* help you. I love you. I don't want you to be hurt anymore."

"There would be terrible hurt done to many if you were to come. Do not ask me again." His gauntlets pressed against her temples. "Please don't make it more difficult for me. Accept this—accept this—*you must accept this.*"

"I don't want you to be killed!"

"You are . . . so selfish," he replied gently.

Her hands sprung away from him, and she whirled back. "Go on, then. Let your gods light your eighty-mile path to hell. They'll burn up there for the next billion years and never know you've lived or died!"

He stared at her with leaden eyes for a moment, then turned and walked away, floated away on the green shimmer of sand, and disappeared into the islands.

She cried easily enough now; there was little relief in that. And after she had wound out her frustration and bafflement on a long run of privately released emotions she returned to the complex.

She had not tried to follow M'landan for either apology or surreptitious protection. All the emotion, all the anger—precipitated from the feeling of being slighted, of being thrown into the deep stream of events with no guidance, no sense of direction, no way to manipulate through the current—all this spun roiling around a center that had remained stable and unaffected, that had, all the while, conceded to the steady judgment that had reached the decision to go to Klada.

In the long hours that followed, she considered what had driven her to send him off in the way she had, considered the elements of herself that remained from the years before, the residue of the person trained to determine with logic and precision a counter action to any given event, and of the suppressed, erratic, and microscopic elements of emotion that had broken off and collected in some centuries-duration Brownian movement within herself, and had risen up in one disastrous wave to sink her in anger and frustration. And as much as she deliberated, approached the subject from every aspect, the echo that fell away cried *pride*. It had certainly led her along that tunnel-visioned course, and when she wasn't engaged in some work at the dwellings, where the running reevaluation of herself still ticked along beneath the physical exertion and parallel with the conversation, she sat on the bronze cloak —that garment which was no longer a reminder of her other life—sat staring into space, the analysis continuing in its slow and painful way.

M'landan had been gone twelve sunfalls when Darenga was attacked by a group of Ilanuians led by Treaden.

She had been showing four of the weavers where some of the plants were located on the plateau, plants that she was familiar with and that seemed to fill the requirements for cloth fiber, most of them roots which had to be dug up from the sand, but she knew of one shrub which had a broad and hollow fibrous stem which flourished in an area along the shadow line, and she had left the weavers digging the roots while she went to gather samples of the shrub. She was kneeling down, to study a stem she had crushed on a broad flat rock, when she heard one of the weavers shout.

She glanced up, saw her waving frantically and calling out a song of alarm that was quickly joined by the others. Darenga swung her head around toward the islands, saw Treaden and some ten or twelve M'dians with him advancing on her. She stood up slowly, revolving on the balls of her feet, taking in all the scene—the weavers some sixty yards from the cavern entrance, but moving hesitantly in that direction; the wide semicircle of Treaden's group already within ten yards of her and contracting the distance, carrying in their hands short silver poles. They stopped as she completed the slow turn and stood facing them.

She waited, judging their stance, the way they held their poles weapon-like, the attitude of Treaden, so obviously their leader. From that deep center of herself came the caution: *don't harm them. Don't resist. If the change is to be made, it must be now*. And instead of repositioning her body, balancing her weight, letting her hands fall casually to her sides, ready, she straightened and slipped her arms into her sleeves. Her eyes moved calmly over the group to settle on its leader.

"Treaden," she asked in a mild tone, "why are you here?"

"Why shouldn't we be here? These are our fields. The better question is why are *you* here? What right do you have here, thief?"

"The Yarbeen is no one's property, Treaden."

There was a motion from the figures to encircle her. Instinctively, she took a backward step, and they quickly hemmed her in. She stood silent. There was a pause, some glances, ultrasonic communication.

They're so afraid of me; every contact they have with me is saturated with fear. Aggression and fear have never been part of their culture. I've contributed to this.

"What do you want from me, Treaden?"

136

"You stole our food," he replied, and it occurred to her then that their finding her was a surprise, that Treaden was being forced by this circumstance into the role he was assuming.

"The food was never used by us. It was left where you could find it," she answered calmly. "It does belong to everyone, you know. Your parents harvested it for all of you."

"Can you imagine this!" the figure closest to Treaden exclaimed. "She's telling you about what our parents did! Treaden, check her hands—maybe she really is one of us."

"Not if she eats flesh," said another.

"What kind of flesh do you eat?" said the first one again. "Priest's flesh?"

"Shut up, Botor!" Treaden said roughly.

"Are you still following a priest who takes a flesh-eater to Chaeya, Treaden?" Botor sneered.

"Don't be foolish!" bellowed Treaden.

Darenga, listening to the subtleties she could pick up in this exchange, said quietly, "You have even more arrogance than L'Hlaadin thought, Treaden."

"Be silent!" he cried.

Confusion and distraction had permitted him to speak to her in that manner, and, realizing this, she said nothing more, but stood waiting as the circle narrowed, Treaden's outburst and her mild response swelling their confidence so that Botor, his weapon braced between his hands, now stepped forward.

"Let's take her to Trolon; he'll have something to say to her about theft."

At that, Darenga turned abruptly, and the suddenness of her move drove the figures who had grouped behind her apart in surprise. She walked away from them toward the weavers who clung to the entrance chamber, tense and ready to bolt, saw them disappear like prairie dogs into a burrow as a rush of sound came up behind. She bent her shoulders to the poles, threw up her arms to protect her head as the M'dians struck at her.

"Trolon will want her!" she heard Botor cry. "Don't let her get away."

She stumbled as a rock hit her on the forehead, and she went down hard on her hands, blood clouding the vision in her left eye. Someone yanked her hood back, and she crossed her arms over her head.

"Look at her!" Botor cried. "Are you afraid of her now? She won't hurt you!"

"No, I won't hurt you! I won't do anything to you!"

"See? Look at this!" And Botor hit her across the shoulders.

She put up her hand to prevent him from striking her again, and he grabbed it, pulling her off balance so she had to clutch his wrist to keep from being swung around by her own body weight onto the ground.

There was a sudden silence, heavy and abrupt. She heard a deep throaty phrase from Botor, and then he pulled her other hand free and dragged it toward him.

"No!" Treaden yelled, and Botor simultaneously cried out with equal force, "Why not? This is no Chaeya—no holy bride of the priest! What do you care?" And he locked his fingers down over her wrists.

"You don't know what you're doing!" Darenga cried out.

Treaden, horrified, sprang forward, but Botor was bent toward her, immobilized. Then his hands slid back, spilling liquid as they released her. She turned her palms over slowly, and the remaining laanva showered into the ground as Botor stared down at her with dull eyes, watching her bury her hands in the green sand and bring them back up cleansed.

"You've made yourself ugly to the sight of every person who has called you brother," she said, coming to her feet. "And now you've dishonored and insulted the one who loves you most, the one who remains to care for you even after your assaults on him."

She swung around. "And you, Treaden; this is the way you repay his forgiveness. When will you feel you've received your full measure of revenge on him?"

Her eyes swept the group. "I'll tell you all this—L'Hlaadin will not be with you much longer, and when he's gone no priest from Klada, or anywhere else, will be able to help you."

She swung back to Botor. "I forgive you for what you did to me, but it's not my forgiveness you'll need."

She turned, then, and walked away unchallenged.

It had all been so natural, what she had said and believed as she was saying it. And she had returned no violence. Everything was still intact. *Ana-il'ma.* She had given him what no one else could, and received in return what was only now becoming tangible.

She had already forgotten the M'dians who stood silent and shaken behind her, forgotten the throbbing over her eye until, as she descended the chain ladder into the chamber, she slipped and came down in a jarring crash on the floor. She pulled herself upright and leaned her forehead against the cold metal links.

How much time have I left? A year? Two years?

The chain clanked dully against the wall as she rocked it slowly back and forth.

Have I given enough?

"Chaeya!"

Darenga straightened, turned around to Klayon and Tlaima, who crowded in behind him, and the weavers behind her, and others behind them in the corridor. Klayon touched her head. "Give me water," he said to someone—not Tlaima, who had sprung up the ladder to look out over the plateau.

"Are many hurt?" Klayon called up. And then to Darenga, "Are they badly hurt?"

"No one is hurt. I didn't touch them."

Tlaima looked down. "They're all standing near the shadow line," she told Klayon.

Darenga gently pulled away from Klayon's brisk ministrations. "I'm all right," she said. "Thank you," and she walked out of the chamber and down the corridor past the weavers.

"We thought they were trying to kill you, Chaeya," one of them said.

"You didn't have to worry," she answered. She stopped, turned.

"Klayon!"

"Yes." He had hurried after her and was immediately behind her. "I did not mean to sound unconcerned about you—"

She waved her hand slightly. "I know your first obligation is to your people, even if they—"

"Not more than to you, Chaeya. You are one of us, too. I . . . worry about your . . . soul."

She stared at him, seeing the consternation, hearing all

139

the tonalities. She bowed her head deeply to him in silent acknowledgement of his concern. Then she said, "Would you please see that Treaden and the rest are given quarters and made comfortable when they come down?"

"Are they coming?"

"Yes. I don't know how soon. But they'll want to see L'Hlaadin. Tell them he'll be here before long. Botor may want to see me. I'll be in my room. Will you see to this for me?"

"Yes, certainly, Chaeya."

She bowed her head again, then continued down through the corridor.

She had been sitting cross-legged and immobile for hours on the cloak when Klayon asked her softly if he could bring in fresh water.

"Yes, thank you," she answered, raising her head.

Tlaima entered with him and stood at the edge of the cloak while Klayon set the water container on the ledge.

"Is there something you wanted to say to me?"

"Treaden and the others have come down."

"I see," she nodded. "Have you given them something to eat and drink?"

"Yes. And they have been given rooms," Klayon answered. And then, after a little pause, "Can you tell us where L'Hlaadin is, Chaeya?"

"Yes. He went to Klada."

"*Klada!*" It was a tortured and involuntary cry that came from Tlaima.

Darenga looked up at her for a long moment before she said to Klayon, "Will you leave us, my friend? I'd like to speak to your sister."

Klayon looked at them both, and then quietly left.

Darenga indicated that Tlaima was to sit down in front of her, and, when she had seated herself, quietly said, "You are making yourself a widow, and you have no right to do it."

Tlaima drew back, her eyes going suddenly gray as Darenga watched her.

"You accept Klayon's love and give him no hope at all of ever having yours unconditionally. Have you ever thought what it must be like for him to know you hold this love for L'Hlaadin?"

She was silent.

"Do you think all this love you feel for L'Hlaadin has escaped his attention? Be truthful, Tlaima; do you think he doesn't know and isn't troubled by it?"

"I have always loved him," she replied.

"But he doesn't love you in the same way, Tlaima. He has a deep and general love for everyone, and you receive it as they do. Yet there is an additional and particular love he has for you because you have an important place in his life. . . ."

She hesitated, for, as she had been speaking, there had been a slight and delicate movement in the universal glass, a lens almost in focus, a sensation of clarity and strangeness.

"I have never expected L'Hlaadin to love me as Chaeya. It would have been too . . . unlikely."

"It isn't that he wouldn't, Tlaima, or that you're somehow unworthy—he has always favored you, and you know it—but he can't return the love you want from him." She leaned forward. "Don't dedicate this kind of love to him; it's a burden that adds to those he already carries. Give this love to the one who can accept it. Give it to Klayon so together you can—" again the sensation of clarity, of the twisting of the glass "—provide for him what no one else can."

It was significant, this thing she had uttered, these words that rang down the levels of her consciousness and vibrated the foundations of the old world she had constructed. Yet it had no special meaning for Tlaima, who was still reeling from Darenga's initial remark.

"I can't continue speaking of this with you."

"Then speak with L'Hlaadin when he returns. He'll make your way and Klayon's easier."

"I don't know," Tlaima said, distraught, coming to her feet. "I don't think I can talk to him about it."

"But neither can you remain silent any more, can you?" It was quietly spoken, but its impact sent Tlaima floating back and spinning out the door.

"Whose pain will finally be greater," Darenga asked softly, "yours or mine?"

In the silence of fourth sunfall, Darenga lay on the cloak, an image of stone carved by a fraudulent moonlight whose radiance never waxed or waned, but had spread its silent illumination down for over one hundred thousand years, unaltered, radiating on life as well as death, and on the slow evolution of subterranean eyes. Perhaps a change had been effected on the ears: the cupping of hands to recreate that gallery of echoes that filled the dwellings all the waking hours.

No echoes now. Deep silence.

What are the rational thoughts?

The control panel of her console. She could imagine every lighted bar and switch, each screen that reflected the bridge of every other Galaxy in the fleet, the slight motion of her chair as she leaned forward to run her hands in a hundred sequences—a thousand sequences that directed the great ringed ship, the galactic vessel that sang like light along the particle flow of space.

I was the logician, the ancient nominalist—dear God!

Her hands balled into fists and pressed against her thighs.

We never wanted violence. In a system of worlds that strained at peace, that constantly gnawed the restraints that prevented chaos, they had been the ones who had maintained the balance. She counted them off: Beta, Epsilon, Lambda, and the Patrolmen; the four clone Houses that had maintained order for a thousand years with violence only twice; the first violence put down without bloodshed, the second with unimaginable destruction, and her finger had been on every bar—genetic control short-circuited, everything awry, nothing predictable, all out of control.

Where was the rational universe?

All is mutability. All is irrational.

And the Laws. Capital letter, that—Laws.

Are there laws?

Governing a collapsing fold that separates for all time that which exists on either side simultaneously, yes. Not fully understood. Not understood at all. Not understood by Captain Areia Darenga, a Lambda clone of Nakota, Maintainer Province, Northern Hemisphere, Earth.

She sat up. Held out her hands. Stared at them in the dim illumination from the window opening, slowly drew a circle with the finger of one hand on the palm of the other. An irrational universe: every time order was imposed, there was a shift, and the old laws no longer moved the same objects at quite the same rate. Diurnal differences.

Millionths of seconds, measurements by microns. And everything was changed between one press of a bar and its release.

My God! My God!

She lay back down with her hands over her face.

An irrational universe that prolongs life, allows it, threatens it, creates, destroys, consumes, consumes.

I die and am reborn. I die and am come again with the soul of a gnat. The irrational gnat wandering soulless, all forlorn.

A shock. *I expected pain and didn't receive it.* Like water; warm, odorless, unfragrant, impotent. The sudden insight into the buried rage of males whose act of rape is the greatest insult to themselves. Who cannot even perform the function of a drone. Barren uncles in an incestuous house.

Oh, God! Let me rest!

There was a jolt of remembered pain, and she clasped her palms together, sitting up again, burying her face in her hands with a deep intake of breath. She stood up, swaying, unsteady.

"Did I give enough?" she whispered in M'dian, and then repeated it in every language she could remember.

"Oh *God*, was it enough!"

She crossed over to the ledge and sat down, sat looking into the dim room, with her back to the window, staring into the edges and curves of pale light.

I can't see beyond the reality I observe.

What did I sense in the words I spoke to Tlaima? It had been undefinable. Something seen with the rods and not the cones. *But it had its own reality, and if I were to describe it to M'landan, he would know.* He would know. *Ana-il'ma.*

There is that reality, too.

Symbiosis.

No.

Apotheosis.

She stood up suddenly, her skin crawling; burning and freezing at the same time.

One can't be drawn up without the other.

He has seen me and known me, and his love is without measure.

You make me his eyes, and you leave me blind!

His loneliness is without measure.

M'landan, can you hear me!

His name is L'Hlaadin, and he holds the balance; he is the Globe and the Stalk.

"Chaeya?" Klayon called softly.

"Yes, I'm awake," Darenga replied, sitting up.

"Botor would like to speak with you."

She sighed deeply, rubbed her hands down her face. "Have him wait in the other room, please," she told him.

He was gone a few moments, and when he returned he had her alternate robe draped over his arm and carried a laver. "The robe you're wearing is all stained," he said.

He set the things down and turned back to her, and she stood quietly as he took off her robe and began to bathe her. "You haven't slept for several sunfalls," he told her. "You will make yourself ill," he added severely. "I know something about human beings, and in some ways the human body is not as strong as the M'dian."

"Don't grumble at me, Klayon. I'll sleep when he returns."

Klayon was silent, scrubbing away methodically as she slowly turned, and she realized then that the particular combination of gentle touch and gruff comment was his acknowledgement of her conversation with Tlaima. "The water will refresh you," he finally said.

As he was fastening her robe while she stood docile and dreaming, her eyes on the columns beyond the window opening, he asked, "Chaeya, why does Botor want to speak with you?"

She turned her head back and looked at him thoughtfully. "Because he needs courage to face L'Hlaadin," she answered.

"They all do, I would guess. There'll be a long count of sunfalls before any of them are ready for absolution."

"That isn't why Botor is here," she told him.

"No?" He stepped back from her to give her appearance a critical look, then went behind her to retie her hair in place. "What did that one do worse than the rest?"

"He—" There was no phrase for it in M'dian. There were words that described the infidelities of a Chaeya, and words that described the male who would share that grave indiscretion, but there was no term for what Botor had

144

done. "He locked hands with me against my will," she quietly answered.

There was a sharp, involuntary yank at her hair. "What!" and Klayon swept around in front of her. "What!" he cried again. "He must be banished at once!"

"That will be up to L'Hlaadin," she replied in a mild voice.

He paced to the window and back again, and then to the door, his arms out from his sides. "What made him think he could commit this outrage! And Treaden a party to this!"

"It happened too fast for Treaden to do anything. He didn't approve. Neither did Botor, once it was done."

She watched his agitation, feeling remote. "He can't be punished for what he doesn't understand," she said, and Klayon drew up short, a strange expression on his face. "Go get Tlaima, please. I think it'll be easier for Botor if he confronts you before he faces L'Hlaadin."

She waited a space, and then went out into the hallway where Klayon and Tlaima, whose shock was evident in her face, fell in behind. Botor was poised in the middle of the room, his eyes wide and dull.

They entered, and Darenga stopped a few paces away from him. "What did you want to speak with me about, Botor?" she said neutrally, with a soft upturn at the completion of the phrase.

He looked from one to the other, struck dumb.

Darenga waited quietly, with both Tlaima and Klayon motionless at her side.

Abruptly Botor fell to his knees. "I've done an unspeakable thing! One thing more in my life that is more offensive than all the offenses of all the generations."

He didn't look up at her, but kept his head bowed as he reached out groping, until his fingers touched her robe and caught it. "*Mlo saindla*, Chaeya."

"I've already forgiven you," she said with a curious stiffness in her voice which drew Klayon and Tlaima's attention to her. She was staring down at Botor, for when his hand had closed around the material of her robe, she had suddenly seen—no, not seen, that was a response of the eye, but *perceived* that portion of him which lay hidden in the recesses of his thoughts and motives, that movement or intent that quickened the pulse of life that comprised him.

145

She perceived it and knew how dark his spirit was, how ignorant, how little he understood of himself and the strength it would take for him to overcome it.

This is what M'landan sees when he looks at us, she thought. *This is the knowledge he uses.*

L'Hlaadin.

"Tell me again, Chaeya! Tell me again!"

"I can tell you until I have no more voice, Botor, but you'll remain deaf to the meaning of it unless you search yourself to know why you should be forgiven."

That new and awesome perception sensed the disturbance in Botor, sensed it as black air moving through smoke.

"You carry deformity inside you, Botor; you're unhealthy at the root."

She was using an analogy to the disease that had attacked L'M'dia and the M'dian people, and whose threat had lain over the Yarbeen for generations. Botor scrambled back from her, gripping his hands together in terror. She had felt the astonishment in Klayon and Tlaima as she had spoken, felt them simultaneously move nearer to her, until their robes were brushing hers. She turned to Klayon.

"Bring your brother a pallet and some water. He'll wait here for L'Hlaadin."

As Klayon moved quickly off, Darenga told Botor, "Talk to no one and eat no food. Spend these hours examining that darkness inside you. I'll talk with you once more before you see L'Hlaadin." She had reached the doorway when Botor finally spoke.

"I will do these things, Chaeya," meaning, I will do these things for you.

"No," she answered. "You must do them for yourself, if you're to follow L'Hlaadin. And you haven't much time left."

Chapter 12

The cry rang down the cavern, a faint birdsong at first, thin, through the forest of pillars, and then the melody distinguishable, and then the name, "L'Hlaadin! L'Hlaadin!" swelling up in a madrigal that brought Darenga to her feet and out the door to the narrow ledge that leaned out into the cavern.

She stood listening as the cries filtered through the columns. There was a wave of M'dians washing suddenly into the open and up against the dwellings, all looking back toward the way they had come. Darenga's legs were stiff and immediately shaky. She bore down on this lack of control, and then thought, *I feel joy; why should I suppress it?* She started down the sloping bridge, her head turned toward the columns.

Behind the last stand of pillars was motion, and she glimpsed some figures, and then M'landan came through, moving slowly within the dance of M'dians. His hood was back, and she could see his eyes clearly as they swept the front dwelling. But she had already reached the bottom of the bridge, and he didn't see her.

He had not come from Klada alone. At his side was a figure she knew immediately to be Protain, in the pale green and beautifully patterned robe of Klada. Instead of the bands of priesthood, he wore a tapestry of black around his hood. As she watched, he raised his hands and drew back the cowl in a slow and graceful movement.

He was taller than M'landan, and strikingly handsome, his eyes amber-shaded, eyes with distinctive pupils that had widened now until they appeared to be limned in gold. His mouth was straight, but rather than severity, it suggested strength and patience, and even in this light, pale and moonlight cold, his skin shimmered with iridescence. Everything about him suggested great dignity and gravity,

147

and he seemed misplaced in the general uproar that was announcing L'Hlaadin.

Beside Protain walked Laatam, stately, subdued, a figured Chaeya band around her hood.

Close now to tears with joy and excitement, Darenga thought, *He has made a peace; he's brought them all together.* Then it occurred to her that she didn't know what the appropriate behavior for her was in this circumstance, and she didn't want to humiliate him before Protain. She glanced about for Klayon and Tlaima, but that was an impossibility, for the crowd was too much in motion for her to see anyone. Anyone but M'landan, who now saw her. She started toward him, her hands slipping into her sleeves, trying to keep a pretense of seemliness as she was jostled about.

But M'landan had no concern about the protocol for such meetings; he made his own. He simply gave his call, everyone fell back, and he drifted through them to wrap her in his arms.

When she drew back to put her hands on his face, she saw his eyes mark the bruises, the cut over her brow, and before he could speak she said softly, "Later. Believe me when I tell you something good came of it."

In answer, he bent his head and touched her palms quickly with his tongue, then turned and drew her back with him toward Protain and Laatam.

"My Chaeya, Protain," he said simply. "Throughout the cities, she was known as the One-who-far-journeys."

Darenga crossed her wrists over her chest and bowed her head, inclining her body slightly, the gesture of respect of a Maintainer to the Circle, the eight who had governed her. There was no higher sign of respect she could have shown him, that she was showing him, not because of who he was, but of what M'landan had accomplished through him.

"You come to the place where all your generations began, and where all M'dians are brothers and sisters," she said, and raised her head.

"Yes," he answered in a lilting tenor that carved the notes in silver, "it is a fitting place to begin a new trust."

And so M'landan had been right in sending the Greynin home. Darenga and Laatam's eyes met, held briefly. Behind Laatam and Protain there were more Kladaks and more still arriving. Darenga glanced at M'landan, who, having Tlaima and Klayon in attendence now, said, "It has been a long and tiring journey, and we are all hungry and thirsty—" and they were gone before M'landan had finished what he was saying.

The procession moved up the bridge Darenga had just come down, and by the time they had arrived at their rooms cloths had been laid and water and vessels of food were on the ledges. Protain's assistants were ready to pour water and food for him in an elaborate bowl they had apparently brought with them. Another bowl of comparable design was handed to Laatam.

Darenga sent M'landan a questioning look, and he gave her a subtle change of eye color in response. She sat down beside him.

"Are you not hungry?" Protain asked. "I don't think I have seen you eat in all the time we have been together these past sunfalls."

"It is a time of fasting for me," M'landan replied.

Now that the initial excitement was over, Darenga could see how thin his face had become; how tired he looked.

"Protain has generously given us a great quantity of food from his stores," M'landan told her.

"We have an abundance," Protain replied, and Darenga heard the deference in his voice, saw it in his attitude, certainly in the fact that he had travelled this far with Laatam to bring it to M'landan's door.

Tlaima and Klayon entered quietly and stood at either side of the cloak.

"It was kind of you," Darenga said. "Is it being brought into the caverns?"

"No," M'landan answered. "It is being stacked near the entrance, where it will be easier to transport."

That passed without comment.

"And when you are ready for your journey," Laatam said, "there will be more for you."

From Tlaima and Klayon there was a profound silence that told the extent of their shock at the mention of a journey. But Darenga's attention was on Laatam. In that drifting and unmanageable perception, Darenga sensed the darkness that lay beneath Laatam's quiet manner.

"Perhaps we should be shown to our rooms, now," Protain said politely, rising. Laatam came up beside him; the perfect Chaeya.

149

"This way," M'landan said, and fell in behind Tlaima and Klayon as they led them out of the room.

They had selected a cluster which had the water system completed, a group of rooms with a spectacular overlook of the cavern, laced together by a delicately arched bridge. The room for Laatam and Protain had been sumptuously —for the cavern dwellers, at least—provided with rolls of cloth and matting, among which Darenga recognized both Klayon and Tlaima's mats. She gave them a glance, which they returned with perfect impassivity.

When the room had been complimented, Protain turned to M'landan in a pause that heralded an expected response. Darenga looked at him, too, saw him compose himself in the familiar way.

Can I see into you? she thought suddenly, and was as suddenly afraid to try.

It was a prayer of reconciliation he sang, and Protain responded to its phrases in his silvery tenor, M'landan's deep baritone underlying and providing the strength and dramatic force that held it aloft like an airy cloud on the wind. And as much a product of that association than anything else, she later reasoned, she saw transposed on her vision, the brilliant blue and cloud swept sky of Ronadjoun, and smelled, faintly, as if she stood far inland, the tang of salt air.

"All is within," Protain sang at the solemn completion of M'landan's blessing, and Laatam's contralto echoed in counterpoint.

When they reached the hallway of their own cluster, M'landan said, "I'll join you in a minute," and turned aside with Klayon and Tlaima into one of the side rooms.

In a short while he came in, saying, "I should have told them of my vision before I left. They have a right to know. But sometimes I neglect these things." He dropped down on the cloak.

"I'm sure they understand," she replied. "Was Protain right? Have you gone all this time without eating?"

"I could not eat in front of Laatam." He lifted his gauntlets. "It would have been too distressing for both of them. Protain has a dangerous tendency to absorb Laatam's guilt."

"Yes," Darenga agreed quietly, "and she carries a great deal of it."

He gazed at her silently, saw then she was about to pour food into his bowl, and said, "No, just water now, thank you. All I want is water. I'll eat later."

She sighed, filled the bowl with water, and sat down in front of him to hold it as he drank. The feeling of warmth rose between them, was exchanged in their eyes.

"You've accomplished a wonderful thing," she told him. "This is a good beginning. How did you convince Laatam and Protain to return with you?"

"There was not much persuading on my part. It was as I said it would be—Protain did not want to see Laatam's people starve."

"And the Greynin?"

"Everything is not settled in Klada yet. There is an instability." He put his gauntlets alongside her face. "Tell me now what happened to you."

She gave him an account, and when she described the assault on her by Botor M'landan's mouth tightened, but that was all the indication he gave her that he was affected any more by that than by her beating.

"I did not expect this so soon. We must be more cautious. I think I will have our food brought in and guards set at the entrance; Trolon seems to be acting independently of Laatam now." He paused. "And you didn't strike back? Not even at Botor?"

"It wouldn't have served any purpose." She brought her eyes up, away from the cloak. "They're caught up in something they don't understand."

He considered this. "What happened after Botor . . . released you?" It was difficult for him, she could see that— the priest rushing to his responsibilities, the husband to his.

She told him quickly those things he needed to know, explained her isolation of Botor in the room at the end of the hall. At that M'landan was on his feet, with Darenga scrambling up after him.

"M'landan, wait! I told him I would see him first, before you spoke to him." She caught his sleeve, and he turned in the doorway. "He knows the seriousness of what he's done to you. He's so afraid, M'landan." She had her hands on both his arms, holding him. "He's afraid to face you. Let me speak to him first, as I said I would."

"Very well, you will speak to him first, but I will be with you."

She looked up at him. "All right. If that's what you want to do."

The M'dian heard them coming and stood frantic at the ledge. Darenga approached him, feeling M'landan at her back as she saw Botor's eyes held at that point above her shoulders where M'landan's face would be. His eyes went suddenly dull, and again she tested the depth of his self-understanding, found it dark, unexamined; too deep for him to fathom alone, and she felt a compassion for his helplessness.

"Your time has not been well-spent, Botor."

"I tried to do as you asked, Chaeya."

She felt M'landan stir. Botor's eyes went wide for an instant.

How can I get past his fear? That's what's preventing him from doing anything for himself.

"Who am I, Botor?" she asked.

"You . . . you are the Chaeya."

A pulse now to the darkness. A wrong answer, she was sure of it.

"Who am I?" she asked again, the voice of command. "What is the name you call me?"

Extreme agitation, his body poised to flee. *If he runs now he's lost.*

"Oh, please!" he cried. And then, "Flesh-eater; child-eater." Again his eyes on the point above her shoulder, but a quieting of the pulse.

"Your laanva spilled into my hands. Did you think me a flesh-eater then?" The question had come too soon; he was not properly prepared for it, and she knew it the instant she spoke it and saw the darkness inside Botor seethe.

He bolted—swung abruptly toward the door, and was arrested by M'landan's voice.

"My brother," he called softly, so softly the melody was left rocking on the air. It was all he said, but it drew Botor around to finally face him.

"My brother," he said again, "you were taught from childhood to stand apart, to reflect, to consider yourself and your habits of thought, and whether they were of the nature that would keep our small family intact, isn't that right?"

"Yes, my brother."

"And if there were thoughts or habits which you were unable to resist or repel, you were to seek guidance from your priest, is that not so?" Still the same gentle rocking song, drawing Botor slowly toward him, until he stood within the curve of an arm, if M'landan would have raised it.

"The small errors and disagreeable habits of mind accumulate in tiny grains, Botor, until the mass covers our judgment and we don't see wrong as wrong at all, but only as a response to a single event."

"Yes, my brother, I can understand that. I acted on the moment—"

"Which act, Botor?" M'landan gently interrupted.

"Both. When Trolon struck your hands off, I thought it a fitting punishment for your transgression."

"And you were there when the screens were opened to my chamber?"

"I helped open them. I saw it all."

"All?"

"I saw your hands locked to hers—"

"To whose?"

"The flesh-eater's," Botor answered, his eyes hard on Darenga as she listened to the ready flow of question and answer, the swift and skillful press and direction that had led Botor to the point at which she had begun. Only now he was ready. She listened and watched the darkness lighten.

It was over, three hours later, when M'landan said, "Botor, you must rest now. Stay in this room. Do not speak with anyone but us."

He raised his head, glancing to the door as he silently called, then back at Botor, who stood quietly with his hands in his sleeves. "Take some nourishment and water, and then sleep. We'll talk again when you are refreshed."

Tlaima, answering M'landan's silent call, came in with a small jar of plovaan and a bowl, which she set on the ledge. With a slow movement of her head as she turned to leave her eyes held M'landan's, and then she quietly left.

M'landan looked back at Botor. "Sleep well, my brother."

Darenga and M'landan walked back down the corridor to their room, where M'landan dropped like a rock to the cloak. She was immediately beside him, laying back his head, smoothing his robes. "You're so tired," she said. "And you've lost weight."

"A little, maybe. I want to talk to you."

She touched his face, slipped her fingers between the fastenings of his robe so they rested on his skin. He lay his wrist over the hand beneath the cloth.

"Until you began to question Botor, I hadn't realized that you have been changed. When did this happen?"

"All the while you were gone," she answered. "But I was so clumsy . . . unskilled. He wasn't ready."

"It is new to you," he replied quietly. "But tell me, Areia, what were you attempting to lead him to?"

Her eyes searched his face. "To . . . a better understanding of his motives. An admission of the extent of his guilt."

"But to what end?"

"I don't believe I had an end in mind, other than to prepare him to face you. I knew that would be the direction you would take. I was just easing the way for him."

"*Dear Chaeya*—but for *what* were you preparing him, ultimately?"

She was silent and, she realized, unwilling.

"If you are to be a guide," he said gently, "you must know the country you travel and the destination of those you would lead."

"And if I don't acknowledge their destination?"

"Then you are a false guide, and lead those who have trusted you only into confusion."

She lowered her head for a moment, then met his eyes. "I spent several sunfalls . . . reviewing, reconsidering my life."

"That is a good beginning."

"It was agony. M'landan, I spoke to Tlaima." And she told him of the strange sensation, of the terrible significance she felt in what she had said to her.

M'landan had sat back up, listening intently to what she said. Suddenly she was apprehensive.

"You know what it means, don't you?"

"Yes."

"Will you tell me?"

"No . . . I cannot."

She accepted that. They sat looking at each other silently, until Darenga began to speak again, describing in slow, precise terms what she had experienced when Botor had touched her robe. "Is that what you see?" she asked him. "Perhaps you don't actually visualize this darkness."

"No," he answered thoughtfully, "it is not like you describe, although the end result seems to be similar. No, darkness is not what I perceive."

"But it is visual, isn't it? Please tell me; let me know what you see."

He looked at her for a long time before he spoke again. "I see from each present moment every possible path that can be taken in the next moment, and I see it being taken."

She stared at him. "But that would—" She stopped, began again. "The space that would occupy would stretch to infinity."

"Yes. And it occupies time, as well, so it is infinite in all dimensions. But only briefly . . . in an instant I must suggest the path which the one needing guidance should take."

"And this is the result of the . . . exchange between us?"

"No, Areia. This is the *Augmeena*, the Holy Insight of the priests. We are born with it."

She finally said, "It must be overpowering."

"Yes. That is why we are kept removed from all but very structured and supervised contact with others when we are very young. We must be trained to use the *Augmeena* for our own sanity, as well as the safety of our people."

"If you were born with this insight, then what was it you received from me?"

Another silence, and then the slow, thoughtful melody, "A way beyond my gods and my present. But only in the instant of *ana-il'ma*, and only when we touch in the fire. It must be done again and again for me to continue to see. . . ."

She collapsed against her heels in a sudden and dispirited motion, and bowed her head against her fingertips.

He told her in a soft minor key, "I have asked myself why my gods have given you the power they have. Why they have made you my completion when you have no belief in them, when everything moves away from that possibility, and it remains something I cannot understand."

Her head seemed too heavy for her to lift. "I don't know

the answer either." The minor song paralleled the sadness in his voice. "I can't believe in your gods, that's true."

She looked up at him then, at the gentle face and the eyes that slowly dulled as she watched. "But I believe what *you* do is right, that out of this wretched universe you are an inherent good, even though I'm afraid of where that will lead you. Or me."

They reached out to each other at the same time. His gauntlets tightened against her head, the old gesture unsuppressed. She caught his arms. "I may have a year left, not much more than that. Perhaps that's why you can't see—"

"It is a possibility." *I try to accept it,* the interwoven frequencies told her.

She lay quietly down beside him.

It was a little game they played—this deep and quick insertion of his tongue into her mouth and her attempts to capture it, encircle it with her own. He lay on her, light, pressureless, cool, his robe open and enshrouding both their bodies.

"You have a butterfly's tongue," she told him, and then had to describe the proboscis of a butterfly, and then, because he was curious, a butterfly.

"My tongue does coil inside my mouth," he said, and showed her when she asked to see.

"Oh," she exclaimed on an exalted and joyful run of notes, "you are such a miracle!" and meant it only half in jest.

This time, when the soft, flexible, nectar-sweet tongue pushed in between her lips, she caught it with her teeth.

"Aaaoo!" he cried, and slipped down away from her, rolling onto his back as she released him. She came up across his chest and gripped his neck with her teeth.

His laughter shimmered brightly in the room. "Please! Let go!"

But she gnawed mercilessly, laughing, her song garbled. "I am an animal, you know; my species is animal. We eat lovely butterflies like you."

His laughter had gotten all out of control, and that she continued vexing him was only because of the delightful sound it made. Finally—out of a sense of propriety more than anything else, the fact that their frolic could probably be heard down the hall—Darenga let him go. She nuzzled him, as he sank back, and gently kissed his ear membrane.

"From what I remember of Earth's history," he said breathlessly, "you would be descended from the butterflies as well."

"Our mutual ancestors took a different branch somewhere along the line. We went with the lions and the apes."

"And all have teeth?"

"Yes."

He was thoughtfully silent. "A strange thing—eating one another."

"It's a survival mechanism, M'landan. The sort of balance that took millions of years to achieve. It's a very orderly process as long as it stays in balance."

"Are most of the worlds in your Alliance this way? Surviving in this manner?"

"In varying degrees, yes. M'dia has had a curious sort of evolution. Remarkable, really, that there are any of you left at all. It's such a severe dependence you have on L'M'dia. And vice versa."

"No more." There was finality in his tone.

"Will you have enough food to last?" *To last to what?* she thought. *And for what? And to where?* The feeling was strong that there would be a journey, a familiar feeling; the orders received, the cargo loaded, the manifest signed. Now the wait for the assigned TDO—Time of Disengagement from Orbit.

"We can only take what has been given us by Protain, the rest of our needs the gods must fill."

And her thought was, *What will the gods provide when the food runs out?*

Let him sleep! Darenga had signaled to Klayon the first time he had stuck his head in the doorway. But things were beginning to stir noisily now, as first sunfall progressed. And when Klayon and Tlaima had appeared again with the intelligence that Protain and Laatam were rising, Darenga finally relented and stroked M'landan awake so they could bathe him.

He stood up sleepily, and Tlaima slid off his robe which, being already unfastened, drew a quizzical look from her. Klayon began a brisk scrub.

157

"Don't they provide baths for guests in Klada?" he asked.

"I had no time for baths."

"You should have taken the time," Klayon replied, wrinkling his nose. "You might have bathed for your Chaeya."

M'landan turned his head to Darenga with a rueful expression.

"I didn't notice," she said, bending her head to cover a smile.

Klayon grunted. "Love numbs all the senses."

"All the senses!" M'landan cried, crooking his arm around Klayon's neck. "It makes some more acute!" And he pulled Klayon's face against his wet skin.

"Hey, now!" Klayon protested, trying to get free.

"Come here, Tlaima!" M'landan told her, reaching out. "Water, Chaeya! Let's have water for these two!"

"Our robes!" Tlaima exclaimed, drawing back with laughter.

"Robes! Robes! Take them off! Now! Take them off, I say!"

They scrambled out of their robes and fell naked and laughing into his embrace.

"Now the water, Chaeya," M'landan told Darenga. "Here, hold it still," and, as she brought the vessel in front of him, he swiftly blessed it.

Suddenly the laughter was gone, and Tlaima and Klayon stood mute with M'landan's arms about their necks as he pulled their faces tightly against his.

"Pour it over us," he said in another voice. "Pour it over us now," and she saw that he was crying.

She turned the mouth of the vessel down, and the water spilled out, ran in silver down their bodies.

"It is not my will that is being imposed on you," he told them. "There are events in the heavens that are random and unplanned, and there are events that are fixed and unchangeable. I act on one such now: you must be joined. From this moment, in the eyes of the gods and in their meaning, and with the loving blessing of your priest and brother, you are joined."

His voice dropped, a deep vibration now, felt as well as heard. "I love you both beyond what you can understand. And as you are joined to each other, you are joined to me; we are linked together as we are now for all time."

When his eyes raised to hers, where she stood holding the empty vessel, Darenga knew she was the only one who heard the keening edge of despair in his song.

With the exception of Botor, who had been isolated but for contact with L'Hlaadin, Treaden and the rest of his group had disappeared in the general confusion and distraction of Protain's arrival and departure. As a precaution, M'landan had ordered the food supply brought into the passageway of the cavern, so now, for three hundred yards, both sides of the corridor were lined with jars and urns and bottles and racks of vials. It had been a wise idea, for, several sunfalls after the Kladaks had left, the entrance to the chamber was closed. It was done quickly and with no forewarning to the sleepy guard, who ran pell mell down the corridor singing out an alarm that set the whole complex in disorder.

When M'landan and Darenga reached the entrance chamber, they were told the cover could not be raised. Four or five M'dians clung to the ladder, pushing at the wide overhead door, but it was not moving.

"Let me up there," Darenga told them, and they jumped out of the way so she could climb the ladder.

She pressed up against the cover with her hands. It was solid. "They have something on top of it," she said. "Probably one of the big rocks around the entrance. Well, we'll see. . . ."

She climbed further up the ladder and braced her back against the lid. It began to yield. She let it down. "I won't be able to throw it off in one heave," she told M'landan. "I'll need something to wedge in here. We'll have to take it a step at a time."

She waited while stones of various sizes were gathered from the pillared section of the cavern, and then she pressed the cover, inserting the rocks in the widening crack until, with one final heave, there was a heavy scraping roll that reverberated through the chamber, and the door was free and falling back on its hinges.

They found that a large rock, indeed, had been placed over the cover.

"They went to a lot of trouble for this," Darenga said to M'landan as they stood surveying the scene. "Is it psychological warfare, or do they intend something else by it?"

M'landan paused over her translation into M'dian of the term psychological warfare. "I think Trolon is behind this," M'landan answered. "Treaden seems to have become the agent of his wishes, and this was to announce their intention to harm us."

"What do you want to do?" Darenga asked. "This is the only way out of the caverns, except for the mile-long opening further down, but that's an impossibility; the sides are sheer, straight to the surface."

"We will protect ourselves in the best way that we can. Do you think three guards will be enough?"

"I would say five would be safer, M'landan. Three outside, one in the chamber, and one a few meters down the corridor. If they attack, the word can be passed quickly along and the three outside can concentrate on closing the door between the chamber and the corridor instead of trying to warn the complex. It would be a good idea, too, I think, to remove the chamber cover so Treaden can't stage any more of these weightlifting contests. Since you're the only one who can open the inner door, we have that protection, and there's not much they can do to the chamber that we couldn't undo. But the guards should be posted right away. And M'landan," she said as he was turning, "no longer than two hours at a time for each watch. We don't want to be caught by surprise again. . . ."

But they were caught by surprise. One of the three outer guards—Atin—was captured, and while the other two stood, indecisive, at the chamber rim, the guard below them passed the alarm, then went up to draw them back inside with her. They just managed to shut the door on a swarm of Treaden's group who remained to angrily hack at the wall where the opening had been.

M'landan and Darenga rushed to the inner door as soon as they heard the alarm.

"Can you hear anything?" Darenga asked after a moment of watching M'landan standing silent and attentive in the pale glow of the tunnel.

"No," he answered. "I'll call to Atin."

She saw M'landan's throat vibrate, and a sudden agonized look cross his face. "What is it? Is he all right?"

"They've hurt him badly with the knives. I can hear nothing else. Klayon?"

"Nothing," Klayon answered, straining forward as he listened through the door. "He must be brought in, L'Hlaadin; he's bleeding to death."

M'landan looked at Darenga.

"They're probably out there, waiting for you to open the door."

"You are the strongest," he said. "Will you go out and get him?"

"Open the door," she told him, and began unfastening her robe, stepping out of it as he made a series of circular motions with his gauntlets and a sound inaudible to her. The door slid back.

She leaped through the opening and onto the ladder, making a swift but cautious 360-degree observation before she flung herself over the rim and sprinted toward the wounded M'dian. From the surrounding rocks, Treaden's force came forward, skimming along the ground in the curious and rapid gait of the M'dians.

She scooped the injured M'dian into her arms and started the return run, judging the small margin she would have to reach the chamber and to lower him into it. She saw Trolon then—Trolon in an elaborate robe fretted with silver and with a silver pectoral that glinted rhythmically as he came nearer—Trolon determined now to see an end to the cavern dwellers.

Darenga reached the chamber, dropped the M'dian into the waiting arms, said, "Quickly, get in and close the door!" and turned to face the onrushing force led by Trolon.

"Stand where you are!" she commanded with a wide gesture of her arms.

But what checked his forward motion and brought him to an abrupt stop was M'landan, coming up out of the chamber. There was silence, and a hesitation in the attackers.

Darenga stood quietly as M'landan stepped over the rim and straightened, so slowly, so serenely. "I can't protect you," she told him softly.

"You would do great evil if you tried," he answered.

"L'Hlaadin!" Trolon cried, in a tone that scraped Darenga's eardrums. "L'Hlaadin is it? The priest who tore up the generations like ploughmeal? Scatterseed, vile, disgusting murderer of our generations!"

He's insane, Darenga realized suddenly, and in the shifting perception she had of Trolon there were no shadows, only a distorted blankness, as if sections of him had been torn away.

"The murderer of our generations was the one who cut off my hands, Trolon. And the ones who helped him. And the one who stood by your side urging that atrocity." Harsh words and a harsh song that might have been edged with bitterness, if Darenga had not known him so well.

Trolon swept in toward M'landan, his knife drawn back. The others circled in. "You speak her name," Trolon raged, "and I'll harvest you and leave your body to the air!"

"I don't need to speak her name," M'landan replied calmly. "You know well enough who I mean."

M'landan stared calmly at Trolon poised glittering and dangerous in front of him. Trolon's eyes shifted to Darenga; he warbled something, and the nearest M'dians closed in, pressing her away from M'landan. She yielded, stood composed, her arms at her sides.

"You tried once to kill her, Trolon. You think by destroying her you will destoy L'Hlaadin and free yourself of the cries of the children that still live within me. But you cannot destroy a special instrument of the gods, Trolon, and when you seek to tamper with their plan you are bringing down a terrible destruction on yourself, as well as those who mistakenly follow you."

His song was a vast, uncoiling theme that sang against the root. "My brother, I am to leave this planet and there will be no freedom for you or for Laatam for as long as you live, unless you make your peace through me. If you do not, your guilt will burn away what reason you have left. Come to me now, my brother, let me give you comfort—"

"Comfort! In those foul stumps? You're no priest. You're unclean—filthy with your own sin and that abomination you've taken to Chaeya. You talk of peace, L'Hlaadin—peace would come flowing like lumeena to heal the wounds you gave people if you would leave this planet. You think I feel guilt? If you had another pair of hands, I'd rip them from your arms and sing with joy! And Yamth and Baandla would spread their light before me in a path of approval and praise—"

162

"Trolon!" M'landan's voice dropped across his frenzied song.

Darenga made a half-turn in his direction, stopped by the arms holding her.

"Trolon, you are my brother, and the gods have made you my charge. But your own actions now require satisfaction of the irrevocable law against offenses toward a brother-priest. You have not only done violence to me, but also to the gods. Forgiveness must come through me and no other priest. Yet I cannot forgive you unless you've proclaimed your guilt before your city. As long as you are unwilling to do that, you will sear with hatred and have no restful moment until the time you fall on your knees before me. And I tell you that the sacred oil will not cover your body, nor will the gods drain it away at the last sunfall. You will not rise whole and untouched by time to take your place among all the generations that have ever been or ever will be. You will drop into the dust, Trolon, and the winds will sift you into crystal, and there will be no prayer that will make you whole again. And you will be lost forever."

M'landan shifted slightly, and his voice embraced the entire company.

"I will soon have no people but the few who follow me now. But I will go so one that comes after me will call all people his own. Our gods have made me guide and guardian for their purposes. The schooling has been long and the training rigorous. And now, after all the generations, they find us ready. Time is short, Trolon, my brother. Make what you can of it now, before it is gone from you forever."

M'landan took a step forward, and Trolon's knife flashed up to balance across the silver plates on his chest. "One more step, and your blood will warm the sand," he said. "And you know that I will do it."

M'landan made a restless movement; the circle around him contracted. Darenga felt the hands gripping her tighten. There was an instant's full and heavy silence, and then an abrupt, shattering roar from the sky that sank everyone to the ground but M'landan, who had expected it, and Darenga, who recognized it immediately and looked up in wonder at the brilliant blue craft swinging on a wide arc of air, slipping down in a sudden silent glide to the plateau, and coming to a stop in a rolling corridor of sand.

With a high, insane scream, Trolon called his followers back into the islands as an exodus of blue-uniformed figures spilled out of the opening hatch of the craft.

Darenga looked across to M'landan and found him watching her. Beyond him she saw the cavern dwellers coming up out of the chamber, flowing over the rim onto the plain. Then Klayon was beside her, saying, "Your robe, Chaeya," and, "Here, let me help you fasten it," as M'landan stood quietly, his eyes now on the oncoming humans.

The crew from the shuttle craft was alert, cautious, but unhesitating, coming forward in the professional manner they had been trained to, and she thought, *These are my people*, but it was a shock for her to see those faces again: the eyes so small, the mouths grotesquely narrow, the noses sharp. *I haven't seen myself all these years! I'd forgotten what I look like.*

She drew her hands into her sleeves as the leader came forward and saluted.

"Captain Darenga—" Hard, unmusical, staccato, but trembling with control: emotion held severely in check. "Do you want us to go after the attackers?"

She answered in Standard Maintainer with the same grating cadences. "No, Conofficer Randley. They'll keep away, now."

"Captain—Captain . . . we were damn glad to find you alive."

"Areia," said another man, coming forward, "if I may, I'm not under the strictures of my friend here." So saying, he embraced her warmly, and she lowered her head against his to answer softly, "It's good to see you again, Bendi Felix."

"It is . . . remarkable." His expression was gentle, but his Earth-blue eyes carried another message as they searched her face. "What has happened to the peaceful M'dians, Areia? What has caused them to attack with knives? And, perhaps most important, how have you deferred Life'send?"

He spoke in a soft tone whose rhythms now were coming back to Darenga who replied, "And how the hell do you come to be here now?"

He made a little gesture of concurrence. "Let's go into

the shuttle. Then we can sit down and answer all the questions we both have."

She nodded and looked at M'landan where he stood surrounded by his people. "L'Hlaadin," she called, and, as Bendi Felix watched thoughtfully, held out her hand to him.

Darenga had seen it all in a wash of familiarity—the tables and comfortable chairs in the area next to the control room, the small food unit that dispensed catspaw. She could have walked away from it only yesterday.

As they seated themselves, Darenga said to M'landan, "L'Hlaadin, this is Bendi Felix, a member of the Beta House of clones, and a great and respected astronomer."

Bendi Felix inclined his head with an amused little smile. But when M'landan replied, "An astronomer! Ah, to be able to chart the stars and know them as one knows the island fields," the scientist's face came alight at the unexpected and pure joy lilting in his voice. "Well, that's a very gratifying response," he said.

"Bendi Felix," Darenga went on, finishing the introduction, "this is L'Hlaadin, the priest of Ilanu, and my husband."

Randley had quietly entered the room and sat down with them, laying the small manual translator on the table as Darenga had spoken. From the scientist, there was a long and thoughtful pause as he looked at M'landan and Darenga. Then he said, "My congratulations."

M'landan turned his black enormous eyes on the conofficer who sat in stunned and continuing silence. But captured in that stare, Randley finally cleared his throat and said, "Yes, congratulations . . . to you both."

In the pause that followed, Darenga said, "Why have you come back, Bendi Felix?"

He looked at her for a moment before he answered. "The Spinandre Fold has reopened."

"Reopened?" She sat forward.

"Yes! At a distance from the old weir, but apparently still part of the aberration. For the past three years, it has been radical and fluctuating, but there is some stability now. We think we might be able to make it through."

"I see," she said. And then, "But that doesn't explain why you're here."

"I decided to bring back some samples of L'M'dia, Captain," Randley told her, at once taking the responsibility for what had been forbidden. "Not enough to shorten the M'dians' supplies, you understand, but *something* in case the weir closes again. Something for all these years. . . ." His gaze had wandered from her face, but came back again. "When we scanned Ilanu, we could see there was trouble, so we've kept a surveillance on activities for the past few days. We just saw you this morning." He glanced at the scientist. "I couldn't believe it," he said, and then smiled slightly at Darenga. "You couldn't have appeared at a better time, Captain."

"I think it's the other way around."

"What? Oh, that's right." He laughed lightly, became quickly serious again. "We need a pilot, Captain. I came through the old weir twice, but when it collapsed, I wasn't at the controls, you were."

"If you're asking me to leave M'dia—"

"Well, yes, naturally—" he hesitated, looked at M'landan, and then back at her and was silent.

"Chaeya," M'landan said softly, "this is the path we are to take."

He had known. Sensed it? Sensed the ship as it swung into orbit? Or had he *seen* it?

Darenga said slowly, "I haven't been on a ship in years. The same years you've been in command, so your time at the helm. . . . I could give you advice, but—"

"Captain," Randley interjected, "even if you've forgotten half of what you know, it will be ten times more than all the experience I've got."

"I have all the respect for Mr. Randley's ability as a pilot, Areia," Bendi Felix said, "but he has every reason to be apprehensive and to want your expertise. It's a narrow configuration and steady only recently. There's no indication of how long it may stay that way."

Darenga's eyes went to M'landan again. "If we try this, M'landan's people are coming with us."

"All of them!" It was the logistics that impelled the comment from Randley.

"Three hundred, at least. More if they choose to come. And we'll have to take on their food supply; they can't eat ours."

"Certainly, Captain. We can make room."

"All right, then." After a moment, she said more briskly, "The gymnasiums would be adequate temporary quarters for them. Since their food is liquid and stored in clay jars and vessels, the high priority holds of Rings Three, Four, and Six would be safest and should have the necessary binders and racks. This food is irreplaceable, Mr. Randley. For every vessel that's broken, their life is shortened. Make sure all the crew assigned to the loading understand it."

"I will, Captain."

She turned to M'landan. "Protain said he would provide more—"

"Yes. Perhaps a large craft?"

"Send a freighter to Klada," she told Randley. "There will be more supplies there to load." *How quickly I fall back into this. And it's not what I want. This is not my life anymore.*

"Will we need an envoy to Klada?" Randley asked.

"I will go with you," M'landan said. "My assistants will help in any way they can here."

He and Darenga exchanged glances. "I'll go back up to the Galaxy with Bendi Felix," she told Randley then, "if you'll supervise the loading from this end. Have Control send down every freighter and shuttle craft that's available."

"You bet I will, Captain."

"Well," she said rising, "I guess we'll get underway."

Randley went into the other room, and the scientist followed him.

"You said there would be a journey," Darenga said, touching M'landan's arms where they rested inside his sleeves. "Did you know it was to be through the fold?"

"I know it will be to Ambassador Seldoldon's planet," he answered.

She made no reply.

167

Darenga sat in the chair of the Captain's console, her cheek resting against the relaxed angle of her knuckles as she thoughtfully watched Bendi Felix and the ship's navigator, Mr. Ohl, reevaluate a running series of figures coming in from the A stations monitoring the reviving Spinandre Fold. "That opens that quadrant a fraction more, anyway," she finally said.

"If it holds, Areia," Bendi Felix said without looking up. "If it holds."

She glanced away to the zoomer, the giant lens which was focused down on the planet and sighted in now on Klada and the loading that was taking place near the city. Streams of Kladaks were hand-loading the food supply into the freighter that stood by. She had been watching M'landan, until he had disappeared into Klada's haruund with Protain and Laatam. Now she peered down the pattern control terminal on her console to monitor Laatam's movements.

Darenga had reactivated pattern control, shut down these many years, as soon as she had come aboard the Galaxy. Both M'landan and Protain, because of a genetic trait they had in common as priests, could not be detected by the frequency-searching device. But every other living thing could, and Darenga had careful tabulations on Laatam, Trolon, and Treaden, just in case.

The M'dians were on board now, quartered in the two gymnasiums on Rings Three and Six. The jars from the Yarbeen had been securely stowed in the cargo holds. When the freighter lifted away from Klada, that would be the final contact with M'dia.

The serum in his hands kept you alive! Reproductive fluid! Remarkable! Bendi Felix had given her a searching look. *He is a most singular being. But, of course, you know that.*

It had been so easy to slip back into command. The lifetime habits, the demand that she had been trained to answer. And yet, it was different; the shell moving about the nucleus, habit and response, automatic, while the interior held its fire intact.

"At this point, Mr. Ohl," she said, rocking forward and putting her finger on the equations that made up the central part of the configuration, "we'll have to decide which part of the ship we're willing to lose." She looked up. "Mr. Randley, get the inventory of stationary equipment on the upper and lower Ring sections, please, numbers three to five and sixteen to twenty. And a list from the Quartermaster of the supplies in those areas."

"Right away, Captain."

Darenga swung her chair back, with an automatic glance at the zoomer. The line of M'dians had thinned out. "What's the status in Klada, Mr. Lapides?" she asked the communications officer.

"Time of departure is forty-five minutes, Captain."

Randley had said, *We managed to comb together enough equipment from the undamaged repairs holds to get limited radio power, but all our deep space communication capability is gone.*

And she had answered, *They'll pick us up the instant we're through the fold. The Alliance will know we're coming.*

That should surprise hell out of them, Captain.

Yes, Mr. Randley, it'll be a surprise, she had replied.

"Here's the hold inventory, Captain, and the stationary equipment list," Randley told her, feeding a tape into one of her console screens.

Darenga watched the figures swarm down. "Looks like the lower section is it," she said, as the three men leaned over her to read the screen.

"A minimum of loss, perhaps," said Bendi Felix.

Darenga looked up at the navigator. "When it goes, we'll have a sudden loss in mass to compensate for."

"I'll calculate it," he said, and moved back to his console.

If the priest is the sole fertile male, Bendi Felix had asked quietly, as they had sat in his quarters drinking catspaw, *then this generation is the last for the people under L'Hlaadin's guidance.*

Yes, she had answered, looking down into the foaming cup. She sat slumped in her chair, her legs stretched out in front of her, the ankles of her boots crossed. The threads in her uniform glinted and reminded her of M'landan's hood. Two worlds. Two dimensions.

How did he lose his hands, Areia? Bendi Felix had asked, oh, so very gently.

She had known the question was coming. She looked away to the table beside her as she set the cup down, and then brought her hand back, linking it loosely with the fingers of her other hand, a bridge from one arm of the chair to the other.

If you understand that his seed, absorbed into my bloodstream through my hands, is what kept me alive, made me whole again, and that this . . . practice is forbidden a priest with the females of his own species until the proper time when all the children are conceived, then you can understand the fear and anger that his people might have felt if they witnessed this between their priest and someone of another species, especially since his seed is limited and is not remanufactured by his body.

And that was their reaction? Or the traditional penalty?

It was a unique situation. No violation of that law had ever occurred with an alien before. And, too, there was a faction that opposed my living in Ilanu.

And out of this mutual disgrace you were married?

Marriage is the nearest equivalent I can give you. The M'dian term is shoma.

The joining.

Yes. It's a specialized relationship between the priest and his Loved One. Normally, from the union would come the priest for the next generation. She was speaking with studied objectivity. *It is apparently genetic. But of course—*

Of course.

M'landan made me his Chaeya to provide protection for me.

You call him M'landan. I thought his name was L'Hlaadin.

It is. His people renamed him after . . . he was banished from Ilanu. I'm the only one who still calls him by his old name, and usually only in private.

I sense love here; something more than mere protection. You were always a romantic, Bendi Felix.

Perhaps, he had said. *But there is more than one kind of love, and that is not the kind I meant.*

"Here we go, Captain," said Mr. Ohl. "The sudden loss of this mass will tend to pull us down into the matrix. The compensation should be this figure, no less than this figure."

They double-checked the calculations with Bendi Felix, then she punched them into her computer display. "Well, it will be there when we need it."

"Captain," the communications officer called, "the freighter is approaching Number Four bay."

"Thank you, Mr. Lapides. Have L'Hlaadin brought to my quarters as soon as he's free."

"I'll relay the message, Captain."

Darenga, the navigator, and Bendi Felix were monitoring the incoming A station data and making minor adjustments in their calculations when Conofficer Randley came into the control room.

"Everything is loaded and secure, Captain. Everyone is aboard."

"Were there any problems?"

"Not a one. We picked up two more M'dians in the shadow line."

Darenga straightened. "Do you know their names?"

"I have them here. . . ." He pulled his scribe unit from his tunic pocket. "Quanti and Samar," he told her.

She rested back against the cushion of her chair and stared at him for a moment. Then she asked, "Where's L'Hlaadin now?"

"In the Ring Three gym. He wanted to see that his people were settled before he came up."

"Did you assign someone to show him the way to my quarters?"

"Yes, I did, Captain."

Darenga came to her feet. "We leave in eight hours; I suggest we all get some sleep."

Her quarters were not far from the bridge of the Galaxy, and as she rounded into the last corridor she came on M'landan and a lieutenant who was escorting him. He gave her a chime of greeting and came forward, slowing again as he saw her uniform.

"Thank you, Lieutenant," she said quickly, and, as they were in front of her quarters now, she opened the door and swung inside, saying, "In here, L'Hlaadin," and shut the door behind him, coming immediately into his embrace.

"Do you know how glad I am to see you? To know you're safe?" She kissed his throat and stroked his face. "Do you know how much I love you, L'Hlaadin? Do you know how incomplete I've been?"

And M'landan listened to this lilting torrent of notes with his cheek pressed against her hair, listened with eyes that were brilliant, that reflected, like a perfect mirror, the room beyond her shoulder.

"And this is where you've always slept?" M'landan looked over at her from where he sat propped against the headboard with pillows at his back.

She wrestled her own pillows into shape. "Yes, whenever I was aboard this Galaxy." She glanced at her chronometer. "Six hours left."

"So soon." He lay his head back in a weary gesture. "Ah, Chaeya, there was nothing I could do for the ones who remained; nothing. There was nothing I could do to make them realize that Protain cannot be their salvation."

"But Samar and Quanti came."

"Yes, I must be thankful for that." He was silent for a moment. "They are all so frightened; it is a terrible experience to fly into the stars, to leave behind our lovely planet that has been our world for all our generations, to leave behind our gods."

"Leave behind your gods, M'landan?"

He turned his head toward her. "And I am the most frightened of all. There is a new voice I hear with the voices of my gods, a new and powerful voice that speaks with words I only half understand. I am . . . floundering under this power." The melodies so complex, the range broad and fading in and out of her hearing, distorting the meaning to her, leaving her unable to respond.

Trying to understand the connotations and significance lost to her in his song, she searched his face and found it glossy with uncertainty. She lay her hand on the damp skin and said, out of her own sudden fear, "We will make it through the fold, won't we?"

"Yes. I didn't mean to frighten you. We will pass through safely." His gauntlet stroked at her hair. "Areia, you must have the ship take you to the place where your life can be extended."

"That will be up to the Alliance. Our orders will come from them."

"But they will allow you—"

"Of course."

"I . . . my love for you is very deep, Chaeya. There can be no one else, for all my life."

Her mouth felt stiff as she spoke. "I realize that; I know it." *But why do you tell me now, and with that sad melody? What is it that you know?*

But the question was never framed to him, because he asked to be taken into her arms then, and she put out of her mind what was only now coming to the surface.

"Bring it up two degrees, Mr. Ohl."

"Got it, Captain."

Darenga glanced at Bendi Felix. "This is like finding your way down a snake hole."

"It has narrowed considerably," he replied.

"Has the reading changed on our trouble point?"

"Only fractionally."

"Mmm."

They had been rooted to their consoles for the past six hours, constantly monitoring the fold they were passing through, the fold that surrounded the ship like a twisting and uneven tunnel, invisible except for the figures that poured down their screens in an endless column, charting the great ringed Galaxy ship down a strange and vagrant reality.

But what would happen if your ship should touch the sides of this tunnel? M'landan had asked her.

Bendi Felix could probably do a better job of explaining it to you, but I'll try to give you a clear explanation. The matrix—in this case, the sides—of a fold have the curious property of being able to absorb the atoms of any mass that enters it. So if a portion of a ship enters, as this one will, it will simply disappear into the matrix. Another curiosity of a fold is that at the point where it's sheared off the remaining surface of an object will be left incredibly smooth and polished, to a degree no known instrument can achieve.

And you cannot see this terrible and dangerous matrix?

She shook her head. *Everything looks just about like it does right now.* They were standing at the long, narrow port in Darenga's quarters. *There will be a difference in the star groups, of course, but it will be essentially the same—clear, undisturbed. The fold will not be apparent, except in the figures. The danger is only visible there. . .*

"Starboard four degrees, Mr. Ohl."

M'landan had entered quietly, and seated himself to one side of the steps leading down to the captain's console, politely refusing the signaled suggestion from a crew member that he take one of the chairs at a console that was not being used.

He watched Darenga through the membrane that had closed over his eyes against the brilliantly lit control room, watched her as she sat leaning to one side, her fingertips braced at her temple, relaxed, the gleaming leather of her boot resting on her knee, rocking the chair with a slight rhythm as she scanned her instruments and quietly gave her orders.

"We're riding the swells, Mr. Ohl. Now steady."

"Just like a roller coaster, Captain."

Bendi Felix leaned over to her, pointed at the second screen he monitored, a screen whose figure column was wildly fluctuating. She stared at it for a moment, straightened.

"Mr. Larus," she said to the flight engineer, "we have three minutes to clear personnel from the bottom ring sections thirteen, fourteen, and fifteen, and top ring sections six, seven, and eight. Get those sections sealed off. Mr. Randley! See to the warning, please."

Her voice was calm, her manner deliberate and cool, but M'landan saw the change in her radiation, saw the growing pulse of fear.

"Clear everyone off the first third of all Ring sections," she called to the flight engineer after another glance at the screen. And to the scientist beside her, "The adjustments, quickly!"

"It's occluding," he told her in a low voice, and M'landan could see his fear, too.

174

"No!" she whispered fiercely. "It can't!"

M'landan rose up then, and asked her, "Why do you say it cannot?"

She spun around in her chair for an instant, saw him standing directly behind her, and swung back to her instruments.

"Captain?"

"Three degrees down, Mr. Ohl."

You said we would get through, she answered M'landan in a fast running phrase.

And you believed in what I said?

Yes. "Three degrees down, Mr. Ohl; it's going to be close."

"We'll wiggle through, Captain."

He has confidence in you, and why are you afraid if you believe in me?

The passage is closing; it's closing on us.

Then you have never believed me.

I believed you, but the instruments don't lie! Dear God! What I believe doesn't affect the physical universe!

Areia, M'landan said then, in notes that fell like broken glass, *I must follow you.*

And in that instant, she came to her feet and bent forward, suddenly on fire, white heat at the center of a blinding blue radiance perceived only by M'landan. She was burning, crying out in pain, as she stared at the universe lying beyond the wide transparent portal of the bridge, at the pale and shifting draperies of light that marked the matrix of the fold. Her hands glowed into the panel as she guided the ship forward, screaming, incoherent to everyone but M'landan who would not yet release her, and to Bendi Felix who could not look away as, at near the speed of light, the ship burst from the weir and into the calm and homeward reaches of open space.

THE FALL OF WORLDS TRILOGY
BY FRANCINE MEZO

The FALL OF WORLDS trilogy follows the daring galactic adventures of Captain Areia Darenga, a beautiful starship commander bred for limitless courage as a clone, but destined to discover love as a human.

THE FALL OF WORLDS   75564 $2.50

Captain Areia Darenga is brave, beautiful, intelligent and without passion. She is no ordinary human but part of a special race bred for a higher purpose—to protect the universe from those who would destroy it. For without the blinding shackles of human emotions, Areia can guard her world without earthly temptations. But when she leads a battle against a foe, Areia finds her invisible control shattered—her shocking transformation can only lead to one thing—love.

UNLESS SHE BURN   76968 $2.25

A tragic battle in space has transformed Captain Areia Darenga into a human and leads her to a death she would have never known. Exiled to the hostile planet of M'dia she lives in the desolate reaches of a desert, struggling for a bleak survival. But then she is rescued by M'landan, a handsome alien priest who awakens in her a disturbing passion and mystical visions of a new and tempting world.

NO EARTHLY SHORE   77347 $2.50
(Coming in March 1981)

Captain Areia Darenga has found life-giving passions in the arms of M'landan, high priest for the M'dia people. Forced from their planet, M'landan and his people are threatened by an alien race who seek their total destruction. As they are mercilessly tracked across the universe by their enemies, Captain Areia, M'landan and his people search for a world where the race may be reborn.

Available wherever paperbacks are sold, or directly from the publisher. Include 50¢ per copy for postage and handling: allow 4-6 weeks for delivery. Avon Books, Mail Order Dept., 224 West 57th St., N.Y., N.Y. 10019

AVON Paperback

Mezo 1-81